REDEMPTION
at Creekside

REDEMPTION
at Creekside

KEITH A. NONEMAKER

WestBow
PRESS
A DIVISION OF THOMAS NELSON

WestBow Press books may be ordered through booksellers or by contacting:

WestBow Press
A Division of Thomas Nelson
1663 Liberty Drive
Bloomington, IN 47403
www.westbowpress.com
1-(866) 928-1240

Because of the dynamic nature of the Internet, any web addresses or
links contained in this book may have changed since publication and
may no longer be valid. The views expressed in this work are solely those
of the author and do not necessarily reflect the views of the publisher,
and the publisher hereby disclaims any responsibility for them.

Certain stock imagery © Thinkstock.
Any people depicted in stock imagery provided by Thinkstock are models,
and such images are being used for illustrative purposes only.

Scripture taken from the King James Version of the Bible.

ISBN: 978-1-4497-7046-4 (e)
ISBN: 978-1-4497-7047-1 (sc)
ISBN: 978-1-4497-7048-8 (hc)

Library of Congress Control Number: 2013901575

Printed in the United States of America

WestBow Press rev. date: 2/13/2013

To the Lamb that was slain and has
redeemed us to God by his blood.

CHAPTER 1

CREEKSIDE

CREEKSIDE IS A TYPICAL SMALL TOWN, the kind that people barely notice as they drive through. The farms and orchards that surround the town are comically referred to as the "suburbs" of Creekside.

The town was founded by two gentlemen: Michael Slater and Alexander Gibson. Perhaps they were not gentlemen though. There was a legend that the two men feuded for a while over the naming of the town. Slater thought it should be called Slaterville, while Gibson thought that Gibsonville sounded nice. As a compromise, so the legend goes, they finally decided to forgo their individual immortality and chose the simple but descriptive name of Creekside: descriptive, but not imaginative. Most towns are built near a creek or other flowing water. After all, water is one of the essentials of life. It's also been an essential of commerce, and for a town, commerce is life. Anyway, the agreement on the town name made peace between them. And it proved a good omen, for even today, Creekside is one of the most peaceful towns you can find anywhere.

The creek is a source of entertainment for the town, but not through ordinary activities. It's true that the kids love to swim in it. And some of the men like to fish in it, although they rarely catch any fish big enough to keep. There's an old joke about how the creek is not good for fishing but it's good for drowning worms.

The real excitement of the creek is the occasional flood. Now and then, a severe storm causes the creek to rise and overflow its banks. The town park gets covered in water: the picnic pavilion, the basketball court, the tennis court, and some of the parking lot. The town itself is on higher ground and has never suffered flood damage. When the floodwaters recede, dozens of volunteers gather to shovel the mud out of the park and back into the creek. Sometimes there is some reasonably good-looking topsoil that has washed down from the farms to the north. Many of the volunteers bring buckets in addition to their shovels, and some of that excellent topsoil finds its way to people's gardens.

After the flood and the cleanup comes the chatter. The big flood becomes a topic of conversation for six years. It's a standing joke in the town. If you misplace something, you say, "It must have got washed away in the big flood." The grammar is not quite right, but that's the way they talk in Creekside. The chatter goes on for six years. Then in the seventh year, give or take a little, there is another flood and the cycle starts all over again.

The park is the venue for the annual Harvest Fest, which is scheduled to coincide with the end of the apple harvest. Almost everyone from the town and the surrounding farmlands will show up during Harvest Fest, and a large percentage of them will indulge in an apple dumpling. Others will enjoy a hot sausage or some fresh-cut french fries.

The town itself begins at Second Street. There is no First Street. The original town plan called for one, but then someone noticed that it would have been in the flood plain. The driveway through the park occupies the space where First Street would have been. Second Street is mostly lined with older houses, many of which are now divided into apartments. Hank lives in one of those apartments.

Third Street is the business district. The north end of the street is home to offices, such as the insurance agency and the doctor's office.

This is also where the public buildings are located: Town Hall, the police station, the fire department, and the library.

The south end of Third Street is the shopping district and is referred to as "downtown." The stores are mostly family businesses. The big stores are the pharmacy, the grocer, the hardware store, and the department store. There are also two downtown restaurants. Maggie's Diner is a sit-down restaurant. The other, The Quick Grill, is mostly for takeout, although there are a couple of small tables there too. There is a movie theater, a Laundromat, and a game room where the kids hang out. The business district is split by Third Street, where there is angle parking next to the central grass strip.

Tucked in between the major stores are a number of small shops. There is a clothier, a florist, and a bookstore. The Bookworm is a quaint-looking building that could easily be confused for a Victorian-style home were it not for the sign above the front door, which bears an image of a cute caterpillar wearing glasses and holding an open book.

The owner, Mr. Stauffer, had been an English literature teacher at a small college. He never could get used to the fact that most of his students needed an English credit on their transcript and their interest in literature went no further than that. After a few years of teaching, he decided to pursue his dream of sharing literature with other book lovers.

One of those was Amy. When someone needs to find her, The Bookworm is a good first place to look. She made a game of finding some obscure novel by some obscure author and asking Mr. Stauffer what he knew about it. Rarely could she stump him.

Creekside had only reluctantly acknowledged the arrival of the twenty-first century. In many ways, it remained old-fashioned. One time a representative of a national department store chain visited the town to do a feasibility study. He asked a number of downtown shoppers, "Would you appreciate the convenience of one-stop shopping in a big, new, well-stocked superstore?" One respondent said, "Well, go ahead and build the darned thing if you must, but I won't be shopping there. I like downtown." The agent must have gotten a number of similar replies, because after he left, nothing more was heard about the project.

The residential area starts at Fourth Street. The houses come in an assortment of styles and sizes. Interspersed among them are several churches and a number of mom-and-pop shops. Amy lives in a bungalow on Sixth Street in a quiet neighborhood.

The state road forms the western edge of the town. Folks call it the bypass. The ice cream shop and the Burger Barn are situated here to take advantage of the travelers passing by the town. Beyond the bypass are some farms. Beyond that is a tree-covered ridge that becomes quite beautiful when the leaves turn color in the fall.

Creekside is a picture postcard of a town—except for one block on the north end of town near the shirt factory. That's where Danny Boy's Tavern is located. The "Tavern" in the name makes it sound more sophisticated than it is. Danny Boy's is a bar. They are said to have great buffalo wings, but to test that rumor would involve enduring a good deal of noise and tobacco smoke.

Danny Boy's also has a pool table and a couple of pinball machines—not the video games that you find most places, but the old-fashioned mechanical pinball machines, complete with the metal balls, rubber-coated flippers, and plenty of noise.

Danny Boy's was also the best place to buy drugs, or so it seemed. Nobody ever caught anybody in the act of selling drugs, but the occasional possession arrest usually took place nearby. There would also be an occasional arrest for drunk and disorderly conduct, or someone might start a fight and get arrested for simple assault.

But that's enough unpleasantness from that one block. The town as a whole was safe, peaceful, and friendly. Amy was fond of saying that Creekside was either serene or boring, depending on your point of view. The exception was that one September …

CHAPTER 2

THAT SEPTEMBER

BILL WARREN, THE MANAGER OF THE PHARMACY, pondered the situation. That summer, things had been tough all over. The economists called it a natural part of the business cycle. Bill saw it a little differently.

Business cycle indeed. That makes it sound like a ride on the merry-go-round. Who pays an economist to say such things anyway? For those of us who work for a living or have to make a payroll, it's more like a ride on the rickety, old wooden roller coaster: you're never quite sure that it will hold together long enough to finish the ride.

Creekside was at least partly insulated from the ups and downs of the national economy. The shirt factory was the big industry in town, and people continued to need shirts even in hard times. In fact, Creekside shirts were high quality, the kind someone would want to wear to an important job interview. That helped delay the effects of the "cycle." But this recession was a bad one, and eventually the shirt factory had to lay off some workers. The shirt makers were the ones who watched the movies, ate at the sit-down restaurant, shopped at the fancy specialty shops, and generally spent money on nonessentials. So when the shirt makers were laid off, those other businesses had to lay people off too, which made more people who couldn't buy anything other than the bare essentials. The cascade effect soon had the whole town hurting. And it really was the whole town that was hurting. Even those not directly affected certainly had a friend or relative who was. That's how it is in small towns; the churches in town cooperate for many good causes. That summer, they decided that a food bank would be needed.

One business always did well when the economy went south: Danny Boy's. There is nothing out of the ordinary about that. When circumstances are bad, plan A is to change the circumstances. But that is not always possible. Plan B is to forget those circumstances for a while. That always spells good business for the bars, usually for the drug dealers, and sometimes for the movie theaters.

Mr. Warren could greet half of his pharmacy patrons by name, which is impressive considering just how many names that was. He made a point of talking with his customers whenever time permitted. He was among the most respected citizens in the town. He served on the school board and contributed liberally to charity. He really liked people. He knew the faces of just about everyone in town.

Bill enjoyed his work, except for one thing: now and then, when things were in a slump, he would have to cut the hours of one of his employees. This was one of those times.

Things were even worse this time than they had been in previous business cycles. Mr. Warren stayed in the store late into the night on Friday, trying to figure out how to make the numbers add up. He had already cut his own pay. There just wasn't any way around it. He would have to cut one job completely. One by one, he went over his payroll list in his mind.

Roland Stockton, licensed pharmacist. That's an easy call. I can't very well run a pharmacy without the pharmacist. Liz Sanders, cashier. I guess that should be cashier and public relations officer. People come in just to talk to her, and when they do, they always buy something too. I hate to do it, but I'm going to have to let one of the kids go.

He called them kids, but they were young men working their first real job. Hank Bauman was a good worker, and smart. If someone came in asking what to take for a headache, he could rattle off the options as quick as a wink: aspirin, acetaminophen, ibuprofen, naproxen sodium. He could tell you the plusses and minuses of each one. He even knew about a lot of the herbal remedies and supplements.

The other option was Jack Powell. He was a pretty good worker too, but a bit slower. He had also called in sick several times, but not enough to merit any disciplinary action. Jack had one big advantage going for him: seniority. Bill always had trouble with this kind of decision. He hated to be the bad guy, so he would often fall back on one of his rules of thumb. He had many of them stored in his brain. In this case, the rule was "last hired, first fired." Rules have the advantage and the disadvantage of being inflexible. Rules will speed up and simplify the decision-making process. But that doesn't mean Bill's decision was easy. He pondered a bit longer, hoping that he would see some way around it. No such luck. Tomorrow he would thank Hank for his service and tell him that he was sorry but had no choice. He would still pay Hank for the whole day.

Bill tossed and turned that night. It was a hot night, at least for so late in the season. Labor Day, the unofficial end of summer, was long gone; and the official end of summer, the autumnal equinox, was quickly approaching. It should have been cooling down, but it hadn't been. The previous night had been exceptionally hot, a last vestige of a lovely summer that didn't want to quit. But that wasn't what kept Bill awake.

Today I have to fire Hank. No. Today I have to lay Hank off. It is a layoff. I have to be sure to make that clear to Hank.

He had to keep reminding himself. Hank was being laid off, a victim of a generally weak economy. He was not being fired for cause. Hank was not being fired for anything he had done or failed to do. He had to make sure Hank understood that. He was a good worker and would get a good recommendation. But Hank was also a hothead. Bill didn't quite know how Hank would handle the news. Once in a while Hank would fly off the handle with little provocation.

Being fired … I mean laid off … might trigger a melodramatic reaction. I don't want a scene in the store in the middle of a busy day.

Hank arrived a bit early and immediately started stocking the shelves. Bill was in his office. The office was elevated above the sales floor. That gave him a good view of everything that was happening. Hank was stocking the dental care area in aisle three. He did everything exactly right. He hung the brushes on their proper hooks; then the dental floss. He neatly stacked the toothpaste, making sure that the new stock went behind the old so that nothing would remain on the shelf long enough to go out of date.

Bill sighed deeply. It was time. He couldn't put it off much longer, and if he tried, it would only make it more painful. Finally, he spoke into the intercom. "Hank Bauman, come to the office please. Hank Bauman."

In a moment Hank was there. "You wanted to see me Mr. Warren?"

Mr. Warren gave another deep sigh. "Hank, I want to thank you for the good work you've been doing."

"You're welcome."

"Unfortunately, the economy is not in good shape right now, and we have to find some way to cut our expenses."

"Oh no!"

"I'm sorry, Hank, but we have to lay you off. I hate to do that to you, and I have every hope that things will improve soon. Then we'll be able to rehire you."

"No! No! I've been doing my work well. You owe me better treatment than that. You can't do this."

"I'm sorry, Hank, but I have to."

"What about Jack? You cut his job and you can save some money. You won't even notice he's gone."

"I'm sorry, Hank. He was hired first. He has seniority."

Hank's face was turning red. "What difference does that make?"

"That's the rule. Last hired, first fired."

Oh no. I did not want to use the word fired.

Hank pounded a fist on Mr. Warren's desk. "No! You can't do this. You owe me."

Mr. Warren had not expected such an intense confrontation. He knew that Hank could be a hothead sometimes, but he always calmed down pretty quickly. Bill had been trying to speak gently. He was trying to show Hank some compassion, which he felt Hank must need at the moment. He thought to himself, *Why is Hank saying that I owe him? I've paid him for his work.*

"Here's what I owe you, Hank. This check covers your hours up to and including today. I'm not asking you to stay any longer."

Hank grabbed the check and held it in a clenched fist. He opened the office door and stepped out. He looked back and said in a loud voice, "You owe me, and you're going to pay." Then he slammed the door behind him and brusquely walked out of the store.

Roland Stockton, the pharmacist, stepped out of the adjacent break room, where he had just poured himself a cup of coffee. He stuck his head into the office.

"Mr. Warren, are you all right? What's all the yelling about?"

"No, I'm not okay just now. I'm shaking like a leaf. I had to let Hank go. I wasn't expecting him to go nuts, at least not that bad."

"He's a hothead. He'll settle down and he'll be fine."

"I hope so," said Mr. Warren.

CHAPTER 3

THE HEIST

It took a while for Mr. Warren to get over the unpleasantness of the morning. He tried to do some paperwork but found himself sitting there and staring at the paper, which, for some strange reason, was not filling itself out. Finally he decided that it would be more useful for him to stock the shelves. It was Jack's day off, and he had just laid off Hank, so there was nobody to stock the shelves. Normally that would be a problem. Lately, though, business had been so slow that there were very few empty spots on the shelves in need of filling.

Mr. Warren decided to fill the "as-seen-on" shelf. That's what he called them: "as-seen-ons." They were all those clever inventions bearing the words "As Seen on TV."

I can't believe my wife calls these things man toys. That's wrong on several counts. First of all, some women buy them, not just men. Besides, these are hardly toys. Take, for example, the wallet made entirely of duct tape. How did mankind survive before this vital item was invented? Then there's the hat that holds a cell phone so that you can talk hands-free. And the spring-powered spoon. You wind it up and hang it on the soup pot, and it stirs your soup for you.

These were great items for the pharmacy. They were usually

bought on impulse or as last-minute gifts for holiday gift exchanges, so they were rarely returned. And the profit margin was pretty high.

Bill was trying to keep his mind off of the events of the morning and was beginning to have some success. He stocked a few other shelves. Then, around six, he went down the street and bought a cheeseburger for supper.

After supper, he took another look at his pile of paperwork. The rules of physics were not cooperating with him that day. The paperwork still hadn't done itself.

Newton's first law of motion: a piece of paper at rest tends to remain at rest and does not fill itself out.

Bill took a deep breath and plunged into the paperwork. Somehow he managed to dig his way to the bottom of the pile. Along the way, he discovered another principle of physics. Staring at the clock multiple times does not make it go any faster. It might even make it go slower. Nevertheless, closing time had finally arrived.

Bill checked the aisles and saw no customers lingering. He talked to Mr. Stockton briefly.

"Mr. Stockton, can you lock up tonight? I've got a headache, and I'd like to get home."

Stockton replied by saying, "You've come to the right place. We have ways of dealing with headaches."

"No thanks. I just want to get home and put my feet up, and I'll feel better. I may even go straight to bed."

"Okay. Suit yourself. I'll make sure everything is locked up."

Bill went to the main checkout, where Liz was counting out her drawer. The small bills and coins would remain in the drawer. Bill put the large bills in the night deposit bag. He would drop it in the night deposit at the bank on his way home.

As Mr. Warren was stepping out of the door, he heard some kind of racket at the back of the store. It seemed to be coming from the restroom area. He paused to try to figure out what the noise was.

Then someone came out of the restroom. He walked a few steps and then began running full speed up the first aisle. He was wearing a ski mask. At one point, he bumped against a shelf, knocking a good bit of merchandise to the floor.

Mr. Warren started to pull the door shut from the inside to stop the guy. Liz screamed, "Look out!" but the guy ran full speed right at Mr. Warren and hit him with a shoulder block. In a split second, Mr. Warren went flying to the ground, hitting his head on the sidewalk. The masked man grabbed the deposit bag and ran down the street. Liz ran out the door to see which way he was going. He ducked into the alley. He was too fast and too far gone for her to try to catch him.

Liz turned back to Mr. Warren. "Are you okay?" He wasn't okay. He did not respond. She reached to turn his head with her left hand. When she touched him, she felt a warm puddle. Her eyes confirmed that it was blood.

Mr. Stockton came running forward from the pharmacy window. "Running" might be an exaggeration; Mr. Stockton was past his prime and not very spry, but he was hurrying. "I called 9-1-1," he said. "The police are on their way."

"You better call them back and tell them to send an ambulance too," said Liz.

But before Mr. Stockton could respond, a police car had pulled up. Creekside doesn't get a lot of 9-1-1 calls, even on Saturday night, so they were able to respond immediately. "Can you call an ambulance?" asked Liz.

"You got it," said Officer Wilkins.

Officer Wilkins pressed the button on his radio—the tiny speaker and microphone were attached to the front of his shirt—and said, "Dispatch, can you send an ambulance to the pharmacy stat?"

"Yes," replied the dispatcher. There was a pause of a few seconds, although it seemed much longer. "The ambulance is on its way."

Officer Wilkins knelt down beside Mr. Warren. "Mr. Warren, can you hear me?" There was no response. Turning to Liz, he said, "Can you tell me what happened here?"

"As we were closing the store, a robber charged out of the restroom, shoved Mr. Warren to the ground, grabbed the deposit bag, and ran. He went through the alley there."

"Okay. We'll take care of Mr. Warren first, and then we'll need to get a statement from the two of you. Can you stick around for a few minutes?"

"Of course."

"Bill, can you hear me?"

No response.

"Has he said anything since he fell?" asked Officer Wilkins.

"No. I think the fall knocked him cold." said Liz.

Turning to Mr. Stockton, Officer Wilkins said, "Do you have a towel or washcloth or something?" Mr. Stockton seemed confused.

Liz said, "Dishcloths, aisle 5A."

Stockton ran—it really was a run this time; the adrenaline must have been pumping—and came back with a handful of dishcloths. Officer Wilkins pressed one against the wound, and then placed another on top of that. "This does not look good," he said. "He's losing a lot of blood."

After a few interminable seconds, the ambulance came roaring up to the store. Matt, one of the paramedics, was out of the ambulance door almost before the ambulance was stopped. He carried a first aid bag with him. "What do we have here?"

Officer Wilkins said, "Head wound. Lots of bleeding."

"Okay," said Matt. "Let's leave the cloth in place and tape over it. Can you hold that steady for a second?" He stretched some adhesive tape across the wound in one direction. Chuck, the other paramedic, had scissors ready and cut the tape. It was obvious that these two had worked together for a while. They moved almost as a single unit. They added another line of tape perpendicular to the first. *Snip.* "Officer, can you hold this again?"

The paramedics pulled a stretcher out of the back of the ambulance and set it next to Mr. Warren.

"Okay, hold his head steady while we lift him onto the stretcher," said Matt. "On three. Ready? One, two, three!" The three men were acting in concert, as though they were one. "Hold him still. That's it."

The stretcher rolled over to the ambulance. Officer Wilkins continued to hold Mr. Warren's head steady until a couple of pillows were put in place. Then the stretcher legs were folded, and the stretcher slid into position.

"Thanks," said Matt. "I'll take it from here."

"How does he look?" asked Officer Wilkins.

"Critical."

By that time, Chuck had packed up the tape and scissors and had tossed the bag into the ambulance. He came around the back of the ambulance and slammed the doors shut. Then he hopped into the driver's seat and they were off, siren blaring. Officer Wilkins turned to Mrs. Sanders. "What did you say your name was?"

"Liz Sanders. Elizabeth Sanders."

"Mrs. Sanders, could you do me a favor? Could you unbutton my shirt sleeve and roll it up?"

Liz gingerly rolled the sleeves. The officer's hands were covered with blood.

"Give me a minute while I go wash my hands."

Officer Wilkins went to the restroom. A couple minutes later, he returned.

"Okay. Can you tell me what happened?"

Mrs. Sanders went through the whole story: the masked man, the shove, the snatch and run. She gave her estimate of the height and weight of the masked man.

"You're sure it was a male?"

"I think so. I can only judge by his size and the way he moved."

"Do you have any idea who the masked man was?"

"No," said Mrs. Sanders.

"Yes," said Mr. Stockton. "I think it might have been Hank Bauman."

"What makes you think so?"

"He was employed here until this morning. He was laid off. I overheard the conversation in the office. He was obviously upset and spoke threateningly."

"What did he say?"

"'You owe me, and you're gonna pay.' Something like that."

"Okay. Let me call this in. Then I'll need a more detailed report. Can you stay a bit longer?"

"Sure."

"Okay." He clicked the button on his mike. "Dispatch?"

"Go ahead."

"We have a four eighty-seven at the pharmacy. We also have a possible assault, although it may have been an accident. The manager was critically injured. The suspect is about five-eleven, one hundred eighty pounds; hair color and eye color unknown. There is a possibility that the suspect is Mr. Hank Bauman."

Mr. Stockton said, "His first name is actually Henry."

Officer Wilkins clicked the mike button again. "Make that Henry Bauman."

The local TV station monitored the police radio channel, and it would soon announce the robbery.

CHAPTER 4

ON THE RUN

MOMENTS AFTER THE ROBBERY, Hank came running home to his apartment. The porch was elevated—three steps from the sidewalk. He took the steps in one jump. He entered the apartment and turned on the living room light. He grabbed the remote and turned on the TV. The show was one of those one-hour detective stories. It was already well underway. Hank didn't care much about missing half of the story. He really just liked having some sound in the apartment. It seemed awfully quiet and lonely without it.

Then a news bulletin came on: "Creekside Pharmacy was robbed this evening. Police are looking for Henry Bauman, a.k.a. Hank, for questioning. Details at eleven."

Hank winced as if in pain. "Oh God, no!" he said. It was the closest thing to a prayer that had crossed his lips in years. *Why am I—Oh, me and my stupid temper. I shouldn't have yelled. Now what? Where can I hide? I'll figure that out. But I can't be here. Gotta get out fast.*

Creekside was a small town, and he knew there was no place he could go in town where he would not be recognized. He turned off the TV and the light, pulled the shades, and peeked outside. There was no sign of trouble yet. But he couldn't let anyone see him. It wouldn't take the police long to find out where he lived. He had to get out of there, and fast.

He pondered his options, and there weren't very many of them. He tried to think of a friend or relative who might hide him, but nobody came to mind. He knew he couldn't drive to another town, as the police would be looking for his car. He decided that the best course of action would be to head for the hills—literally. If he could remember the survival skills he had learned in the Boy Scouts all those years earlier, he could live in the woods for a while until he figured a way out of this situation. But he didn't have any equipment, not even his Boy Scout knife. He then remembered that his uncle was an outdoorsman. He shortly decided to go to Uncle Phil's house and borrow some equipment.

Quickly he sneaked out the back door and traveled through the alleys as quietly as he could. When he got to his uncle's house, he found that no lights were on inside. He then remembered that his uncle was going to be out of town that weekend. That was just as well. He wasn't sure that his uncle would help him if there were a police chase involved. That would have made his uncle an accomplice, and he was not the kind of guy who would willingly break the law, not even for a relative.

Hank knew that the camping equipment would be in the garage. He looked through the garage door window, but it was too dark to see anything. The door was locked. He felt around the doorframe, thinking perhaps there was a key hidden somewhere.

No such luck. Must have got washed away in the big flood.

He wondered if there might be some way he could get the door open—a credit card or a coat hanger—but there just wasn't any time to spare. He took off his coat, folded it neatly, and laid it against one of the glass panes in the garage door. Then he swung his fist hard against the coat. He hoped that the coat would muffle the sound and protect his hand from being cut by flying glass shards. It worked well on both counts, but the glass did cut his jacket. Somehow, seeing his high school jacket torn was an emotional last straw. Tears filled his eyes. As he wiped them away, he said, "Oh God, no." It was his second prayer of the day, and probably only the second in the last ten years.

He shook the jacket hard to dislodge any glass fragments that might have stuck to it. Then he put it on again. An all-terrain vehicle was parked neatly in the center of the garage. He checked. The keys were in it. He remembered that his uncle had said a while back that if he ever wanted to take it for a spin, he should just say the word. So he said out loud, "I want to take it for a spin." This was certainly not what his uncle had in mind, but desperate times call for desperate measures. Where had he heard that expression anyway? It didn't matter.

He knew it would be helpful if he could see what he was doing, but he didn't want to turn on the garage light, as it might attract some attention from the neighbors. Fortunately, his uncle was a well-organized guy. He figured the flashlight would be someplace where his uncle could find it in the dark. He checked the shelf closest to the door and closest to eye level. There it was. It even worked, but it was kind of dim. There was no telling how long it would last. He decided to switch in new batteries, which he found right next to the flashlight.

He went about collecting everything he needed. From somewhere in the remote recesses of his mind, he remembered something about a hierarchy of needs.

Air, water, food, and shelter, in that order. Air won't be a problem. It better not be a problem. You can't carry a box of spare air with you. Water. Water.

He spotted a large, empty water jug. On the side of the house was a water spigot with a hose attached. Evidently someone had been watering the grass. He disconnected the hose and filled the bottle, which he then chucked into the ATV.

Food. Food. I could have grabbed something out of the fridge at home. Too late now.

He looked around. There was no food in sight. He did find a hunting bow and a few arrows. His uncle had showed him how to use the bow a few years earlier. They had only shot at paper targets, not moving ones. Still, he guessed that he could shoot something and cook it if he had to. That meant he would need some matches to start a fire. He looked around and found a baby food jar, tightly sealed, with a few wooden matches inside. Into the ATV it went.

Shelter was the next concern. He figured there must be a tent somewhere, but he didn't see it. He did spot a couple of sleeping bags on the shelf. He grabbed the darker one, figuring it would be harder to spot.

Anything else?

He saw an emergency survival kit backpack, so he grabbed that too. He didn't know what was in it, but he'd worry about that later. It was time to get running now. He had a moment of panic when he remembered that he would need a key to drive the ATV. He didn't know how to hot-wire a vehicle.

No, I already checked that, and it's in the ignition. You're about to do this. Have you forgotten anything? You better think of it before you open the garage door. You might attract the attention of the neighbors, so you want to get going as soon as the door opens.

He saw a baseball cap hanging by the door. He decided to put that on. It would cover half of his face, making him harder to recognize. He also grabbed a pair of work glasses, the kind made of shatterproof plastic, and put them on. If anyone did see his face, he would be "the guy with the glasses," and that was not Hank Bauman. Hank Bauman didn't wear glasses.

He started the engine, pressed the garage door opener, and backed out into the street. He drove off as quickly as he could. He tried to hurry without looking like he was hurrying, as he did not want to attract attention.

His childhood penchant for exploring might come in handy now. He knew all the back roads.

He wanted to avoid the main roads, where he was more likely to be spotted. The farms that were situated between the town and the mountain were served by a narrow gravel road that ran more-or-less parallel to the state road. By taking that road, he avoided the better-traveled state road for a couple miles. He had to get back on the state road, heading north, for a mile or so before he turned left onto the county road. This took him up and over the mountain. Then came the tricky part. If he remembered correctly, there was an old fire road just over the crest of the mountain. But he didn't even know if it still existed, or that he would be able to spot it in the dark.

He slowed down and looked carefully. He did not see it. Then he grabbed the flashlight and shined it at the woods. There it was. It was hidden by a new growth of weeds at the side of the road, but that had to be it. He backed up a few yards and then made a sharp left onto the fire road. The going would be bumpy from here on.

After about ten minutes of steering around the bumps and gullies, he came to a split in the road. The fire road continued to the right. To the left was a remnant of an even older road that was overgrown with weeds now. Maybe it had never been a road at all, but it was wide enough to have been one. He maneuvered the ATV up this road or path or whatever it was until it was well hidden in the foliage. This was the end of the road for the ATV, both figuratively and literally.

He threw the emergency backpack over his shoulders and slung the bow over his shoulder too. He had grabbed several arrows but no quiver to carry them in, and they were awkward to carry. He decided that he really only needed to take one. If he missed on the first shot, his prey would take off and he wouldn't get a second shot. He stuck the arrow between the folds of the sleeping bag. He stuffed the flashlight into the sleeping bag too, as well as the jar of matches. He stuck the sleeping bag under his right arm. He grabbed the water jug with his left hand. This was not going to be fun. That jug was kind of heavy. Had he missed anything? He wouldn't need the hat or the glasses. He left them on the seat of the ATV.

Now he was off to try to hike over the mountain. He had crossed the mountain from east to west in the ATV. Now he was going to hike over the mountain from west to east. Illogical, but he hoped that it would confuse the police and throw them off of his trail.

The moon was three-quarters full, so at least it wasn't pitch black. Still, it was dark enough to be dangerous. There might be a loose rock that would collapse from under his foot; a rabbit hole that he could step in, causing him to break an ankle; or a sharp stick that would stab his leg. Even worse, the stick could stab his water bottle and release its contents.

Get back to reality, man. Just take it carefully, and you'll be okay.

Several times, the tear in his jacket got caught on a branch and made the tear worse. He walked for a long time. His sneakers were not meant for walking over sharp rocks, and the water jug had turned from kind of heavy to very heavy. He had no way of knowing what time it was, but he guessed that it must be well past midnight. The moon was now a little lower in the sky, and trees were blocking it out, so he took out the flashlight. Unfortunately, the beam was narrow, so it did not help much with navigating the rough terrain. He guessed that it was about time to stop for the night anyway. He looked around for someplace that could serve as his camp.

How long am I going to be trapped here? I don't even want to think about it.

First he thought he ought to rehydrate himself, so he lifted the water jug to his mouth and took a gulp. The water jug was well designed, but it was heavy. He figured it must hold at least two gallons. If he could remember the conversion factors, he could figure out how heavy it was.

Let's see, a pint's a pound the world around. How many pints in two gallons? Forget it. I'll figure it out tomorrow. Gotta get some sleep.

Drinking from such a large jug was not easy, and he probably spilled a pint to get the pint that he drank.

He unrolled the sleeping bag and lay down, but he felt something jabbing him in the ribs. He had forgotten about the arrow and the matches. He moved them aside and lay down again. There were a couple of sharp rocks beneath him, so he flipped up one end of the bag and dug out the sharp rocks and tossed them aside. He lay down for the third time.

Third time's a charm, right? Okay, this is about as good as it's going to get.

This was not a pleasant bedroom for someone accustomed to a soft mattress, but he thought he might be tired enough that he would fall asleep quickly. That didn't happen. It seems that some of the birds had never gotten the message that nighttime is for sleeping. And then there was the wind. Every gust made a noise of its own, and the stronger gusts sent the trees into a chorus of squeaks and rustles. He decided to count imaginary sheep. He was somewhere north of six hundred when his mind finally settled down and gave him a few hours of peace.

CHAPTER 5

HER

HANK AWOKE EARLY. The sun was just popping its head over the treetops and shining brightly on him. Was that what had awakened him? He didn't think so. But then what had?

Then he heard the crackling of dry leaves and the snap of a twig. Someone was walking through the woods. The steps were slow and sounded as though they were getting closer. His camping spot was hidden behind a thicket of assorted weeds and thorns. Slowly and carefully, he extracted himself from the sleeping bag without making a sound. Then he looked to his right and saw the source of the noise.

About a dozen yards away, he saw a flat spot covered with low grass and no weeds. It looked for all the world like a well-trimmed lawn, but it was hidden deep in the woods. Stepping onto the lawn was a young lady. She had a small knapsack, from which she pulled a beach towel that she spread out on the grass. Then she knelt down on it. She pressed her hands to the ground and wiggled around a bit, evidently looking for a comfortable position. Then she turned her hands palms-up. She tilted her head back and closed her eyes. Her lips moved briefly, as though she were saying something, but if she said anything aloud, Hank couldn't hear her.

She knelt there like a statue for several minutes. There was a trace of a smile on her face, a look of contentment.

As Hank looked at her, in his mind he said, *"She walks in beauty like the night of something something and something something."* He hadn't been able to remember it when it was on the test, and he couldn't remember it now. And why would those words come to him now anyway? This young woman was not a beauty. Not in the usual sense, anyway. She had a rather plain face. Her hair was dark, almost black; and as everyone knows, gentlemen prefer blondes. And if she was feminine in any way, the blue jeans and flannel shirt hid it well.

After a few minutes, she took a deep breath and tilted her head down, as though she were coming out of a trance or something. Then she looked into her knapsack and pulled out a book. She lay down on the beach towel and opened the book to a marked spot somewhere around the middle of the book. For perhaps a half hour, she read from her book. Then she packed up and took off.

Hank had all kinds of questions about her. *Who was she? What was she doing here? Will she come back? Should I move to another spot farther away?*

If he had really thought about that last one, the answer would most certainly have been yes, he should move. This was too close for comfort for someone in hiding.

Anyway, for the moment, Hank's priority task was to get something to eat. And as luck would have it, he found a potential food source very close by: a rabbit's burrow. He would shoot a rabbit, then skin it, clean it, and cook it. Of course, he'd have to start a fire to cook it, but first things first. He soon spotted a nice, big rabbit grazing nearby. It looked like an easy shot.

He loaded the bow and drew the string back. Then he aimed. At that point, he realized that his hands were shaking. He had never killed an animal larger than a fly. He had eaten game meat that his uncle had bagged, and he had liked it, too. But the thought of dealing with the blood and guts was making him nauseated. Slowly, he released the pressure on the bowstring and then removed the arrow from the bow. He took the few steps back to his camp and set the bow and arrow down next to the survival kit.

Now what? I wonder if Tony's Pizza delivers out here. Well, let's see what's in the survival kit. A pocketknife. That's as worthless as the bow and arrow. Some matches, another flashlight, a first aid kit. What have we here? High calorie survival bars. Three of them. That's what we're looking for.

He grabbed one of them. It was wrapped in foil and quite difficult to open. It would have been easier to open had he remembered the pocketknife. He took a bite. It tasted vaguely like granola, although he would more likely describe the taste as "dusty." It was hard and very dry. He had to take a sip of water after each bite. And he repeatedly spilled a bit of water with each sip. He ate about a third of the bar; that would be enough for one meal. The bar satiated his hunger, but not his appetite.

Okay. Now what? I don't suppose there is a TV set in here. Let's see, we have a pencil and a writing pad. I could write myself a letter. Some facial tissues. Keep them handy. They will serve as toilet paper. Going through this pack will not keep me busy for long. Is there a pack of playing cards in here? Nope. Nothing here to pass the time.

He was desperate for something to do so that he would not be thinking about jail, police, and courtrooms. Hank had never been in serious trouble, but some of the friends that he hung out with had. He had gone to visit one of his friends in jail, and he had found it unnerving. And the horror stories that his friend had told him of what went on inside the jail were not pleasant, to put it mildly. He had to get his mind on something else.

The contents of the survival pack were now scattered on the ground. He arranged everything in a way that seemed logical to him. He decided where his kitchen would be and placed the survival bars and pocket knife there. The bathroom was a tree at a sniff-proof distance from his camp. He had already broken it in.

He couldn't think what his next move would be. In fact, he wasn't thinking clearly at all. He hadn't gotten much sleep, and it soon occurred to him that sleep was as good an activity as any other under the circumstances, so he crawled into the sleeping bag and tried to drift off. But thoughts of jail kept creeping into his brain, making it difficult.

Isn't there something else I could think about?

In fact, there was another thought that kept creeping into his brain too: Book Girl.

Who is she? I wonder if she lives in Creekside. She doesn't look familiar, but then I'm not sure I'd even notice her in a crowd. I wonder what she was doing here in the middle of nowhere. Does she come here just to read? If that's all she was doing, she could have just gone to the library. Will she be back again? She acted very much at home in that clearing. It sure wasn't her first time here. What was she reading? Probably a romance novel. Should I move farther away? Maybe I should, but she didn't even glance in my direction today, so I guess I'm safe here, at least until I figure out my next step.

Gradually, his conscious thoughts turned into dreams as he drifted off to sleep. When he awoke, it was about suppertime. Not that time had much meaning where he was. He could draw a clock on his writing tablet and put the hands wherever he wanted. It wouldn't make any difference. Feeling a bit silly, he did just that. He drew a clock set to six o'clock and then said, "Oh look, it's suppertime." He had another serving of cardboard-flavored compressed sawdust, washing it down with copious amounts of water.

He tried to think of a way out of his predicament. He couldn't live in the woods the rest of his life. He struggled unsuccessfully to come up with a plan. There was no way he could turn himself into the police. He finally decided he needed to give his brain a rest.

He had two flashlights, one that had been on the shelf and one that had been in the survival bag. That made four batteries. He took the batteries from the flashlights and spent his evening trying to teach himself to juggle, with little success; but at least he had found a way to pass some time.

The next activity he busied himself with that evening was counting the branches of the closest tree. He was repeatedly stymied by the uncertainty of whether he had or had not counted a particular branch. Not that it mattered. No one would ever check his work, and if his number was wrong, it would make no difference in the bottom line of his company.

What shall I call my company? Henry Bauman Twig Counters, Incorporated.

There is a fine line between silly and crazy, and he could feel himself moving closer and closer to that line.

Maybe I'm already crazy. Maybe the events of the last twenty-four hours never happened at all except in my demented mind.

Darkness finally arrived, and he lay down to go to sleep. Once again, thoughts of police, courtrooms, and jail crowded into his mind. Once again, he used thoughts of Book Girl to drive them away.

CHAPTER 6

DAY TWO

ON HIS SECOND MORNING AT THE WILDERNESS CAMP, Hank awoke early. It must have been about seven, judging from the light in the sky. With no alarm clock, he customarily would have been able to sleep much longer. There was a woodpecker jackhammering at a tree not far away. Maybe that was the alarm clock that had awakened him. He was sort of groggy and not quite sure.

Anyway, I wonder what's for breakfast. Ah, here we have ... leftovers from last night's supper. Filet of fiberboard. All right, so it's not all that bad once you get used to it, but it's so dry! Let's see, does this call for red wine or white wine? Ah, here's some clear wine. That will do nicely. He picked up his water jug and started guzzling from the rapidly dwindling supply.

After breakfast he went to the men's restroom—still just a tree. As he returned to camp, he heard some brush rattling at a distance. He scrunched down onto his sleeping bag and peeked between the leaves. It was Book Girl. She was spreading her beach towel at the same place as she had the previous day. Hank tried to find a comfortable pose so that he could watch her without being seen—and also without getting a cramp; that might have been the bigger problem. He knew he had better not move while she was there so as not to attract her attention by making noise. It occurred to him that he had made a brilliant selection of campsites. It was more luck than brilliance, no doubt, since the entire episode had occurred in the dead of the night. But the spot he had chosen was engulfed in heavy foliage and would not be noticed even from a relatively short distance away.

It was warmer than it had been the day before, and Book Girl had dressed accordingly. Her blue jeans had been replaced with hiker's shorts, the kind with a big cuff above the knee. Her flannel shirt had been replaced with a floral-print blouse that was light in color, and apparently lightweight. Her shoulder-length hair was pulled back into a ponytail. Her routine started the same way it had the previous day. She spread out her beach towel and then knelt down facing up the hill, took a deep breath, and tilted her head back. She moved her lips. This time he could hear a sound come from her lips, but he could not make out what she was saying—or singing. It might have been singing.

After about ten minutes, she tilted her head down and took a deep breath—almost a yawn. She adjusted her position. So did he. But in the process, he shifted his weight onto a twig that snapped. She jerked her head in his direction and stared and squinted, apparently trying to determine what had made the sound.

Hank froze. He needed to divert her attention somehow. He could see the rabbit's burrow off to his right and just uphill from Book Girl. He quickly concocted a plan that just might save the situation—or fail miserably, but he didn't have a lot of options. Being without options can be a great motivator. He looked around for a small stone. He didn't find one, but he did find a hunk of tree bark that might work. He aimed carefully at the rabbit's burrow and whipped the chunk of bark toward it. He missed, but not by much. Instantly, the rabbit took off in the opposite direction. That was exactly what he had hoped would happen, even though he couldn't actually see the rabbit. He looked back at Book Girl. She heaved a sigh of relief and then smiled. He also heaved a sigh of relief, but he had to do it very carefully so as not to be heard.

Book Girl began to unbutton her blouse. Hank's heart started pounding.

This definitely has the potential to be better entertainment than counting branches. Better even than juggling batteries.

As the blouse came off, it revealed the upper half of a two-piece royal blue bathing suit. She took a tube of something from her knapsack and rubbed it on her exposed skin, starting with her shoulders. He figured that it must be tanning cream. Hank's heart settled back into a more-or-less normal rhythm. Book Girl stretched out on her towel. She moved it a bit to catch more sunlight, and then she stretched out again, facedown. She took the clip out of her hair and let the hair fall over her shoulders, half on each side, so that her neck was exposed to the sun. Then she opened her book.

Hank couldn't help noticing that she looked a lot better this time than she had in jeans and flannel the previous day. In fact, she was quite lovely.

Maybe it's the unblemished skin. No, there is more to it than that. It's something more ... I don't know ... spiritual rather than physical. An inner beauty. "She walks in beauty like the night of starry something and something something." And then there's a line about crow-colored hair. Mental note: If you live through this, learn that poem.

After a while, she turned over and held the book above her face as she read. She read a few pages that way, but evidently it wasn't a very comfortable position for reading, for she soon laid the book down beside her. She reached into her knapsack and pulled out a somewhat oversized pair of sunglasses and put them over her face. Then she relaxed for a while. Maybe she was even sleeping. It was hard to tell. Hank looked upon the scene as someone might look upon the Mona Lisa, studying every detail of the picture.

At last, she stirred. In catlike fashion, she stretched her limbs one way and then another. She rolled her head like a gymnast loosening up before the competition. She put on her socks and sneakers and tossed everything else into her knapsack except the flowery blouse, which she put her arms into.

Hank leaned a little to the left to get a better view. Then suddenly his left foot slid out from under him, creating a loud noise. This was followed by an even louder noise as his body plopped to the ground. He had twisted his ankle, and he winced with pain.

"Who's there?" she called loudly. Her facial expression betrayed a feeling of alarm and fear.

CHAPTER 7

CAUGHT

HANK HAD BEEN CAUGHT. If he tried to run now, he would have to leave his gear behind. He started calculating his options. His best bet would be to act like there was nothing wrong.

Two people just happened to run into each other while waiting for a street car—ten miles from the nearest street corner and eight decades from the last street car. I'll have to give a performance worthy of Shakespeare. "She walks in beauty like the night." No good. That wasn't even written by Shakespeare. At least I don't think so. I can't remember who did write it. Besides, it's not the sort of thing that you say to a perfect stranger on first meeting. Well, I had better say something quick.

Book Girl called out again, "Is there someone there?"

"Sorry, ma'am. I didn't mean to startle you."

"What are you doing here?"

"Hunting."

She suddenly folded her arms across her chest, as if to hide her overexposed body. Actually, her swimwear was not particularly immodest. One could see much more exposed skin at a public beach. Nevertheless, she turned around and, with her back to Hank, buttoned her blouse. Then she turned toward Hank again.

"There isn't much to hunt in these woods."

"So they tell me."

"Where is your gun?"

"No gun," he said as he reached for his bow and arrow and displayed them to her.

"Bow and arrow?" she asked.

"More sporting that way."

"Get anything yet?"

"Naw. Shot at some rabbits, but they're too fast for me."

At this point, her facial expression changed. Her eyes opened wide, and her muscles tensed up. Her expression had changed from mild embarrassment to fear, maybe even terror. "You're that guy," she said.

"What?"

"You're the robber."

"I didn't rob anyone!"

"You robbed the pharmacy."

"I didn't rob anyone," he said, more forcefully this time.

"Your picture has been all over the news," she said as she took a step backward.

"Well then, we have a problem, don't we? I can't let you leave here. You'll tell the police, and then I'm a goner."

"I won't tell anyone that I saw you," she said as she took another backward step.

"Swear it."

"No," she said. This was not what he expected to hear.

He said more loudly, "Swear it."

"Do you think I'm lying? If I speak the words 'I swear,' then you'll think I'm telling the truth? I won't swear. You can believe me or not."

"I could kill you right here."

There were a few seconds of tense silence. Then she said, "No, I don't think you could."

"What do you mean?"

"The way you're holding that arrow, you'd be stabbing me with the feathers."

He turned the arrow around and gripped it tightly.

"I could kill you now."

"I don't think so. You couldn't even shoot a rabbit."

"I missed."

"If you had shot and missed, your arrow would have lodged in the dirt. That arrow is spotless, like it just came from the factory." As she spoke, she stepped backward.

Slowly, he lowered the arrow to the ground. "You're going to turn me in, aren't you?"

She exhaled as though she had been holding her breath for a long time. She kept backing away from him.

"I said I wouldn't tell, and I won't."

By this time, she had taken a dozen steps backward. Then, suddenly, she spun around and ran like the wind down the hill.

Now what do I do? Run after her? Retreat further into the woods? Would that even help?

Hank began to run after her, but he had only taken a couple of steps when he realized that the pain in his ankle would make it impossible to catch her.

He was almost out of water. He had a survival kit but no survival skills. Book Girl had run off without her backpack, so Hank dug through it in the hope of finding something that would help him survive. The only thing he found that would be of any value at all was a water bottle with a couple sips of water in it. He immediately drank the water. There was nothing else of value in there.

The day seemed to be interminable. Hank ate some more vitamin-enriched cardboard and drank most of the water. He tried to conserve a little.

Maybe it will rain. Did I learn how to do a rain dance in the Boy Scouts? If so, I can't remember it any more.

Hank juggled his batteries and counted sticks. He tried very hard not to think about the disaster that might await him the next day—or maybe even that very evening.

Uncle Phil would tell me that that's like trying not to think about an elephant.

Hank had tried not to think about an elephant enough to understand just how futile that effort was. But evening came without incident, and that gave him a little hope.

At long last, night fell, and Hank tried to get some sleep. He went over his plan to clear his mind of all his problems so that he would be able to fall asleep. Astonishingly, he fell asleep almost instantly.

CHAPTER 8

AT LAST, SUPPER

It was barely dawn when Hank woke up from a surprisingly refreshing night of sleep. He opened his eyes and was startled. Some kind of glistening metallic monster was towering over him where there had been nothing the previous day. His heart started thumping like a drum. Then, when his eyes began to focus, he saw that the monster that had startled him was a stack of bottled water. There were three six-packs stacked one on top of another. He sat up and looked around. There was no other sign that anyone had been there—not even the knapsack that Book Girl had left behind in her haste the previous day. Hank had scattered its contents when he rummaged through it. Now the backpack and all that had been in it were gone.

By now Hank was talking to himself out loud. He had been doing so for a while without realizing it. "I guess a few days of total isolation will do that to you," he said.

He broke another piece off of his survival bar. He held it in the air and proclaimed, "Breakfast of termites!" He opened one bottle of water and emptied it pretty quickly. He took the next few minutes to complete his walk to the outhouse, and then he settled down for some serious juggling practice. "I wonder if electrons fall out of these batteries when I juggle them."

As the sun was nearing its apex, he heard a noise in the distance. Instinctively he hid behind the brush, although he thought it must surely be Book Girl. Sure enough, Book Girl called to him from a distance, as if she knew that he would be jumpy.

"Hi, Hank."

How does she know my name? She must have heard it on television.

As she got close, within sight, she said again, "Hi, Hank." She was carrying her knapsack in her right hand. She placed it on the ground near the grass plot.

"Hi yourself. I see you were here earlier."

"Are you sure about that? Maybe it was the tooth fairy. Did you count your teeth?"

Hank just smiled. "Thanks. Did you turn me in?"

"I said I wouldn't. I hope you like burgers."

Hank looked at the sack that she held in her left hand. It had somehow escaped his notice. It bore the insignia of the Burger Barn. She pulled a giant sandwich from the bag, a sandwich called the Barn Burner, and handed it to Hank. He dove into it headfirst.

"Thanks for the food," she said.

"Huh?"

"I like to say a prayer before I eat."

"Oh. Sorry."

"No sweat. I'm sure God understands that these are unusual circumstances."

"Anyway, you're not even eating," said Hank.

She reached over and tore a bit of the roll from Hank's sandwich and popped it into her mouth. "I love sesame seeds," she said.

Then she pulled a glass bottle from the sack. The Burger Barn was one of the few places left that sold sodas in glass bottles; it was some fancy brand that you couldn't get just anywhere. "I got a grape soda," she said.

She pulled a knife from her pocket, the kind with a dozen tools built in. She found the combination screwdriver / bottle opener and popped the cap off of the soda bottle. "I hope you like grape," she said. She took a sip herself and then wiped the rim of the bottle with a napkin and carefully placed it beside Hank, making sure that it would not upset.

"Love it," said Hank. He took a swig.

When Hank finished his sandwich, she drew in close to him. She said, "Look me straight in the eye." He complied. "Hank, did you rob the pharmacy?"

"No, I did not. That's the truth."

Their eyes remained locked for several seconds. Then she said, "I believe you, Hank."

"I'm glad to hear there is at least one person on my side."

"The truth is on your side, too."

Hank squirmed a bit to get into a more comfortable position. As he did, his left ankle became visible.

"What happened there?" she asked.

"Where?"

"You're bleeding."

"I scraped my ankle on a log earlier. I didn't realize I had scraped it open."

"Sit down and give me your foot."

"You don't have to do that."

"We've got to take care of that. It could easily get infected. Give me your foot."

Hank complied.

She untied his sneaker and pulled it off. Then she gently rolled his sock down from ankle to toe and then lifted it off.

"This is dirty; we're going to have to clean it up." She grabbed one of the water bottles from the stack, opened it, and poured it over his foot. He winced.

"Does that hurt?"

"No, it's just so cold."

She grabbed a napkin out of the burger bag and wiped the worst of the dirt away. Next she applied more water and wiped again. She then gently patted dry the area around the wound with another napkin.

She reached for the survival pack and pulled out the first aid kit. She took out some antiseptic ointment.

"This may burn a little bit."

As she applied the ointment, Hank winced. This was not a little burn. It stung like the dickens.

"Sorry," she said. "You want another bottle of cold water to put out the fire?"

"No, thanks."

Next she found a large gauze pad and placed it over the wound. Then she got some adhesive tape and taped it in place. She cut the tape with a pair of scissors built into her pocketknife.

"Okay, Hank, that's about the best I can do. I suggest you leave the sock and shoe off for now. Let it breathe a bit."

"You have me at a disadvantage," said Hank.

"What do you mean?"

"You know my name ..."

"Everybody knows your name. It's all over the news."

"You know my name, but I don't know yours."

"Amarel," she said, accenting the last syllable.

"Like the Little Mermaid?"

"That's Ariel," she said, sounding just the least bit irritated, as though she had had to make that explanation too many times.

"Okay. Amarel. I don't think I've ever heard that name before. It's pretty."

"Thanks. My parents said that it means 'the one who loves God.' As far as I can tell, that's only true if you mix two different languages. Anyway, it's a good name. It fits me."

"Religious, huh?" he said with a tad of disappointment.

"I don't think of myself as religious. Religions are about man trying to reach God. I'm a Christian. I think God reached out to men."

"Uh huh." Hank snorted.

"You seem to have a problem with religion."

"I just wonder: if there's a God, why does he let bad things happen to good people?"

"I'm guessing that is a particularly pertinent question for you right now."

"Why isn't God here to help me?"

"What do you mean?" Amarel asked. "He sent you a whole pile of bottled water."

"You brought that."

"Okay, I was the delivery agent. Who says God can't work through people? Hank, I know your situation stinks right now, but don't make a final judgment until all the facts are in. I'm going to poke around a little and see if I can figure out who is responsible for the pharmacy incident."

"Are you so sure, then, that I didn't do it?"

"You're no killer," she said.

"Wait, what do you mean by 'killer'? We're talking about a robbery."

"Well, I guess you missed part of the story. The store manager was attacked during the robbery. He was badly injured. He's in a coma. If he doesn't come out of it …" She paused for a moment. "I'm sorry to add more bad news, Hank. Hey, I have to go. I'll come back and check on you tomorrow. Is there anything else you need?"

"Yeah, a deck of cards. All this idle time is driving me crazy."

"Hold on." She went and grabbed a book out of her knapsack. "This will keep you busy."

"Oh yeah, I forgot. The sixth commandment: thou shalt not play cards."

"The sixth commandment is 'Thou shalt not kill.' It sounds like you're dealing with some legalism. Sorry, Hank, I just don't have any cards. This is the best I can do. You can twiddle your thumbs if you prefer."

"Sorry, Amarel. I didn't mean to be ungrateful. I really do appreciate all you're doing for me. Thank you."

"I gotta run, Hank. I'll come back tomorrow."

"Good-bye, Amarel."

She was already walking away, but she stopped and turned around. "Some of my friends call me Amy."

"Are we friends?"

"We must be. We're already exchanging gifts."

"What gifts?"

"I gave you a burger. You gave me an arrow and a knife." She held up a pocketknife, the same one she had used to open the grape soda and cut the adhesive tape.

Until then he hadn't noticed, but his arrow and the knife from the survival kit were missing.

"Just playing it safe," she said. "You said yourself that you were going crazy. Bye, Hank."

"Good-bye, Amy."

CHAPTER 9

DANGER

AMAREL HAD GIVEN HANK A BOOK called *Where His Feet Have Trod*. He didn't recognize the author's name. He read the dust jacket first. It apparently was a novel based on the life of someone whom Jesus had healed and who then became a believer. It was not the kind of book he would have read normally. He didn't read a lot. When he did read, it was nonfiction, usually history. He'd much rather have a deck of cards and play some Klondike solitaire. But this was the option available to him, so he started reading.

Although he started the book reluctantly, it drew him in. It must have been the way that the characters seemed real: people who had doubts and thought hard before following Jesus. Jesus himself was portrayed as a real person.

Hank had an image of Jesus drawn from stained glass-windows. He had always thought that Jesus had such a bland, lifeless face. Expressionless Jesus leading his sheep. Expressionless Jesus calming the waters. Expressionless Jesus praying in the garden. Expressionless Jesus knocking on the door. But in this book, stained-glass Jesus gave way to a real person. This Jesus got angry. He laughed. He got tired. He enjoyed a meal with friends.

Hank was so engrossed in his reading that he hardly noticed the passing of time until it became difficult to read because the sun was getting low in the sky.

He closed the book, thinking he would finish it the next day. He hadn't thought about food since lunch, but now he realized that he was hungry. He guessed that it would be cardboard casserole for dinner. But his feast was interrupted. He heard someone running through the woods.

"Hank!" It was Amarel's voice. She was out of breath and agitated. Her call was almost like an intense whisper.

"Over here," said Hank.

"Do you trust me?" She said, still running.

"I think you're the only person I trust."

"No time to explain. Grab everything you can carry and get down the hill. Get into the blue car parked down there."

Hank wanted an explanation, but he really did trust her, and she was clearly distraught, so he did exactly as he was told. He zipped up the sleeping bag and used it like a duffle bag. He threw everything into it that he thought he could carry and hurried down the hill. He was unnerved to learn just how close he had been to the road. He had thought he was hiding deep in the woods. Amarel ran the other direction, up the hill. She was carrying a squeeze bottle of ketchup. As he looked back over his shoulder, he saw her spraying ketchup all over the ground about fifty feet above his camp. She then followed him down the hill, carrying the two six-packs of water that he had not grabbed.

As Hank clambered into the passenger's seat, Amarel opened the car trunk, tossed everything into it, and slammed the lid. Then she hopped into the driver's seat and peeled out. "The police are after you," she said.

"Then you better not get stopped for speeding."

She eased off the gas pedal and let the car slow down until she was close to the speed limit. "I don't want to go too much under the limit either. That would also draw attention." She glanced over at him. "How did you get to the mountain, Hank?"

"I borrowed my uncle Phil's ATV."

"Well, he doesn't think it was borrowed. He reported it stolen, along with the camping gear. Someone found the ATV today."

"What's with the ketchup?"

"That wasn't ketchup. It was hot pepper sauce. They're sending bloodhounds after you, starting at the ATV. I'm hoping that a snoot full of pepper sauce will throw them off the track."

"That's pretty clever. But they only would have been able to trace me down to the highway anyway."

"Okay, so I'm not so clever. I don't have a lot of practice driving the getaway car for a hunted felon."

"I don't have any experience *being* a hunted felon either."

"Sorry. Courage, Hank. Maybe together we can figure this thing out."

"Watch your speed," said Hank.

Amarel spoke to herself out loud. "Okay, Amy, you've got to calm down. Stay focused. Deep breaths." She took a long, deep breath. Hank could see that her white-knuckled grip on the steering wheel was relaxing a bit.

By the time they got back to Creekside, Amarel was calm, or at least doing a believable imitation of calm.

"Okay, Hank. I'm taking you to my house. I'm going to send you in the back way so you don't attract any attention. When I stop the car, get out and shut the door as quietly as you can. Go through the yard and down the steps to the basement door. The door is unlocked. Go inside—it will be dark—and wait there until I come in the front. My neighbor usually stops me to chat, so it could take a few minutes. Got it?"

"I think so."

The neighborhood was very quiet that night, so Hank was careful to walk silently. He found the basement door and walked in. The basement was very dark. He thought he saw a washing machine or dryer, but that was all he could see. It seemed to take a long time, but finally Amarel turned the light on and came partway down the steps.

"Hi there. Selling vacuum cleaners?"

"No. Encyclopedias."

"Come on up."

Hank followed Amarel up the stairs.

"This way," said Amarel. "Here's the bathroom. Get yourself a nice, long, hot shower. When you're done, take another one."

"That bad, huh?"

She smiled slyly. "Hey, if you friends can't tell you …"

She handed him a large garbage bag. "Toss your clothes in the bag. I have a couple of errands to run. Should only take a few minutes. If you sing in the shower, set the volume to low."

"You got it."

She turned and was out the door in no time at all.

He closed the bathroom door behind him. Next to the shower, he saw a folding TV tray. On it was a new, wrapped bar of soap. Indeed, almost everything on the tray was apparently new: a washcloth that matched the towels that hung from the towel rack, shampoo, deodorant. Everything was carefully arranged, like an operating-room nurse might do. Nail clipper, toothbrush, toothpaste, mouthwash, floss. Hank wondered if she actually was an operating-room nurse. He couldn't remember if she had said what she did for a living. There was more: disposable razor, shaving cream, and—he had to laugh—a brand-new deck of playing cards.

Hank stepped into the shower. The feeling of the hot water was delicious. He scrubbed thoroughly and shampooed his hair. A couple times he did, in fact, catch himself singing, perhaps a bit loudly. That was something he did frequently, but it was so subconscious that it didn't occur to him that someone might hear him.

When he finally stepped out of the shower, the plastic bag was gone, but a second TV tray had appeared. On it were new packages of underpants, T-shirts, and socks. There was also a pair of blue jeans. It was the only thing in the ensemble that clearly was not new. But they were in good condition and fit pretty well. Just a bit large, but that was fine.

He got dressed, shaved, and brushed his teeth, and then he opened the door. Amarel was sitting in an easy chair in the corner.

"Well look at you," she said. "You're looking quite human."

"Thanks. You look pretty good yourself."

"Your belt and wallet are on the coffee table."

"What about my sneakers?"

"I'll try to wash them tomorrow. They're the only things I think are worth trying to salvage. Meanwhile, you're stuck here for the time being, and you don't really need shoes here. When was the last time you had a good night's sleep?"

"Actually I slept pretty well last night. Ask me when I last had a good meal."

"When?"

"I had a good burger for lunch today. Before that it was quite a while."

"Well, I don't have very much here that I can feed you. You like pizza?"

"Of course."

"It's getting late," she said. "Let me see if we can still get one delivered."

She made the call without needing to look up the number.

"Can I still get a pizza delivered? Cool."

Turning to Hank, she said, "What do you like on it?"

"My favorite is sausage, mushrooms, and extra cheese."

Amarel repeated into the phone, "Sausage, mushrooms, and extra cheese. Oh, and a two-liter Dr. Pepper. Fifteen minutes? Great. Thank you." She turned to Hank. "We just made it."

"Does that count as a miracle?" he asked.

"I've never heard of a miracle pizza before, but God does move in mysterious ways sometimes."

"If I get out of this alive, I'm going to take you out for a real dinner," said Hank.

"I appreciate the offer, Hank, but I'm not sure that would be a good idea."

"Okay. I know you can do better than me."

"Not better in quality, just better suited for me. My faith is such a basic part of me. I'm not going to try to build a relationship with someone who doesn't share that."

"And if I become a Christian?"

"You don't become a Christian to get girls, Hank. It doesn't work that way. If it isn't real, it won't work."

"Okay. I understand. Sort of."

"Did you want me to try to rescue your school jacket? It's pretty messed up, but maybe if we get it dry cleaned—"

"No, it's torn. But I wonder if you could rescue the letter off of it?"

"That we can do. Were you an athlete?"

"Not really," said Hank. "I was second string on the wrestling team but never got to wrestle in competition. That was in my junior year."

"What about your senior year?"

"I had to drop out after my junior year. My father took off for parts unknown, and I had to get a job to support my mom and little brother. I started out flipping burgers."

"We all have had to pay our dues," said Amy. "Are you still supporting your family?"

"No. Mom found herself a boyfriend and moved in with him. I don't see much of her or my little brother any more."

"That's sad," said Amy.

"I was delighted to get the job at the pharmacy," said Hank.

"It's much nicer work than standing over a hot grill all day. Now I have no job, no income, no home. And my family is hardly a family anymore."

"Hey, let's not get morbid. You were looking pretty relaxed there for a minute. There's not much we can do tonight, so let's leave tomorrow's worries for tomorrow."

"Okay. I'll try."

"By the way," said Amy, "when the pizza gets here, duck behind the couch. No sense letting anyone see you here. "

They chitchatted for a while. When the pizza arrived, Amarel prayed: "Thanks for the food."

"Sorry," said Hank, "I forgot about the prayer. I've never heard of anyone using such short prayers."

"Prayers don't have to be long and involved. It's not like you're telling God anything he doesn't already know."

"Are we ready to eat now?"

"Yep."

Hank dove in as though he—well, as though he had had nothing to eat but cardboard for a while.

Amarel enjoyed it too. "Hey, this is a pretty good combination."

When they finished eating, Amarel showed Hank what was where. "Here's the bedroom. You can have the bed. I'll sleep on the couch."

"Oh no, that wouldn't be right."

"No, you need a soft bed after two nights on the ground. I often fall asleep reading on the couch anyway. If you want to stay up awhile, you can sit at the kitchen table and play cards. Do you want me to wake you up in the morning or just let you sleep?"

"I'll sleep, thank you," said Hank. "Hey, what are these lists for?" He was looking at five sheets of paper filled with names and tacked to a bulletin board.

"Those are my prayer lists," said Amarel.

"So why five separate lists?"

"I try to pray for all the people I'm supposed to pray for. For instance, Saint Paul says to pray for those in authority, so my first list is people in authority."

"I recognize the president and vice president. This guy is a supreme court justice, right?"

"Yes."

"I recognize the governor. Who are all these other people?"

Amarel pointed to groups of names. "These are cabinet officers. That's the secretary of state. These are legislators. This is a county commissioner."

"Wow. You get down to the nitty-gritty, don't you?"

"When I hear something about someone on the news, I put them on the list. The second sheet is my friends. I don't need any special incentive to pray for my friends. I'm always happy to do that—"

Hank interrupted. "Now this is the list that caught my attention. It seems I made this list." He pointed to the word "Hank" written in the margin.

"That's my enemies list. Jesus said to bless those who curse you. So I pray for my enemies."

"I see. And that list seems to consist of international terrorists and Hank Bauman."

Amarel silently walked away, found a pencil, and returned. She scribbled Hank's name off of the third sheet and then wrote it on the second. Hank seemed less than totally satisfied with this response. Amarel said, "You have to remember that the first time we met, you threatened my life."

"Yeah, I'm sorry about that. I was in a panic and ... I'm sorry. You've been so good to me, and I really do appreciate it. Thanks, Amy."

Amarel smiled. "Anyway, this list"—she pointed to number four—"is my angel list. It has pastors, missionaries—folks like that. Anybody doing good works for others. The last one is just anybody I think of who doesn't fit one of the other lists. So anyway, I'll need the bathroom for a couple minutes. Then I'll be out of your hair until morning."

"Amarel ... Amy ... I don't know how to thank you."

"We'll figure that out tomorrow as well. Good night."

CHAPTER 10

DOUBTS

When Hank arose the next day, he could smell pancakes. He got dressed and followed the smell to the kitchen.

"Good morning, sleepyhead," said Amarel. "You must have been up late. Did you win?"

"What?" asked Hank.

"Did you win your solitaire game?"

"Oh, no. I mean, I wasn't playing solitaire. I finished reading that book you gave me."

"Oh, really? What did you think of it?"

"Well, it was interesting enough to keep me up half the night. But there were a lot of religious words I didn't understand."

"Like what?" she asked.

"Like 'redemption.'"

"That's an easy one. Do you know what a pawn shop is?"

"That's where you sell your old jewelry so you'll have enough money to buy drugs," said Hank.

"I'm afraid that's probably true more often than not. But that's not the way it's supposed to work. Actually, a pawnshop doesn't buy things. It makes loans. The jewelry or whatever is collateral for the loan. If you can't repay the loan with interest, then they keep your collateral and sell it to someone else. If you want your jewelry back, you have to repay the loan, and that's called redeeming the jewelry."

"Okay, I understand that part, but what does that have to do with religion?" asked Hank.

"You're a sinner. So am I. Our sins put us in debt to God. Most people who get a loan from a pawnshop can't pay it back. We can't pay what we owe for our sins. The only way we can get our life back is if someone else pays off the debt for us. That's what Jesus did when he died on the cross."

"That makes sense, except for one thing," said Hank. "I don't think anyone gives up their life for someone else if they don't have to. I don't know anyone who would do that. The Romans killed Jesus. Besides, I don't think you're a sinner. Not a very big one, anyway."

"There are no big and small sins in God's eyes. Sin is sin."

"Then why are the police after me and they're not after you for whatever you think you did that's so bad?"

Amarel sat down and folded her legs. Hank didn't know it, but this is how Amarel prepared to present an important object lesson.

"We each start out with a white shirt. Sooner or later we decide to dip it in a mud puddle because it looks like such fun. Once you do that, it doesn't matter whether you dipped it in just one mud puddle or many. It doesn't matter whether the puddles were big or small. It doesn't matter whether you dipped it once or many times. All the muddy shirts are the same. Do you understand what I'm saying?"

"So what was your mud puddle?"

Amarel sighed deeply. "I don't really like to talk about my mud puddle. It's kind of embarrassing. But maybe it will help you understand where I'm coming from. Do you know what anorexia is?"

"Is that the binge and purge thing?"

"That's bulimia. It's similar. I used to look in the mirror and see a fat, ugly slob."

"But you're so attractive."

Hank had second thoughts. *Oops. Maybe I shouldn't have said that.*

"Thanks," Amarel replied. "But what I saw wasn't real. It was my distorted self-image. I was lying to myself, and that makes it a sin already. I went without eating for days at a time, trying to lose weight."

"So what happened?"

"A good friend of mine took a picture of me in my bathing suit, from the back. She cropped off the head and feet. She showed it to me. The body was so emaciated, you could count the ribs. I said, 'that's terrible. She's starving to death.' Then my friend told me it was me. It took some work, but I got my mind straightened out."

"That's quite a story. But I don't understand why that's a sin," said Hank.

"The underlying sin is pride. I wanted to be the girl that all the guys whistled at. I was jealous of all the pencil-thin models that you see in the magazines."

"Still, you didn't hurt anyone, so why is that such a big deal?"

"Do you know who Karen Carpenter is?"

"The singer?"

"Yeah. She died of anorexia. I managed to get straightened out in time, but it could have killed me. And as far as hurting anyone goes, can you imagine how my parents would be hurting if they had to watch their daughter starve to death?"

"I'm glad that didn't happen," said Hank.

"I'll bet you are. If I had died then, you'd be dying of thirst in the woods right now."

They sat quietly for a moment.

Finally, Amarel said, "Well, It's time to see if we can redeem your situation. I'm going to poke around a bit and see what I can find out. By the way, I washed your sneakers. They're drying in the sun on the back porch. They should be dry by this afternoon."

Amarel was gone throughout the morning. Hank couldn't go

anywhere, so he played solitaire. He could have read another book—there must have been hundreds of them on Amarel's shelf—but he wasn't much of a reader. He had just finished one book. That was enough for a while. He watched TV a bit, but there was nothing interesting on at that time of day. So he played cards.

CHAPTER 11

THE EVIDENCE

Around lunchtime, Amarel returned home. She was clearly quite agitated.

"Okay, Hank, come with me. We have to talk." She stomped into the kitchen. "Sit."

He sat in the chair she had pointed to. She sat down across from him and looked at him like a prosecuting attorney might.

"You haven't been playing it straight with me. I believed your innocent talk, but I'm not sure anymore. They've got a lot of evidence against you."

"Like what?"

"Did you threaten your boss?"

"I told him he owed me and he was going to pay. That was the day he fired me."

"What did you think he owed you?"

"I don't know. I guess I wasn't thinking clearly. I just felt like it wasn't fair for him to fire me. I worked hard for him."

"Well, you didn't tell me you were fired," said Amarel. "Revenge is a strong motive for assaulting your boss."

"But I didn't assault him."

"They showed part of the surveillance tape on TV. The guy sure looked like you; the right height and weight."

"Could you see his face?"

"He was wearing a ski mask."

"So that could be almost anyone," said Hank. "Lots of people are built like me."

"The ski mask apparently came from the pharmacy's stockroom. Do you know anything about that?"

"We had a few on the shelves last winter. They didn't sell."

"They found your fingerprints all over the shelf where the mask was stored."

"I'm a stock boy. My prints are on everything in that store."

"Several people saw you running into your apartment right after the robbery."

"I was out jogging that night."

"At ten o'clock at night? People don't jog at ten at night, Hank. You'd know that if you were a jogger. I don't think you jog at all."

"Not very often. I was agitated that night. I wanted to burn off some nervous energy."

"You stole your uncle's ATV," said Amarel.

"He told me I could borrow it some time."

"How did you get into the garage?"

"I had to break a window."

"They've got a good case against you."

"But I didn't do it."

"Look me straight in the eye, Hank."

He stared into her eyes. He had seen that look before. It was Amy's lie detector. Hank remembered hearing somewhere that the eyes are the window of the soul. Amy was ignoring the walls that he had tried to build around himself and was staring through the window and straight into his soul. He had been through her lie detector before and had passed the test, so surely he would pass it again.

Amarel said, "Did you rob the pharmacy?"

He spoke slowly and firmly. "I did not rob the pharmacy."

Amarel held his gaze for what must have been a full minute.

Hank broke the silence. "Are you going to turn me in? I can't go to jail. I can't! It would kill me."

"I told you that I wouldn't turn you in, and I won't. But if I find out that you've lied to me, I'll kick you out of my house and you'll be on your own. So if there's anything else you haven't told me, now's the time."

Hank thought hard for a moment. "I've stolen candy bars at the store—two or three a week almost since I started working there."

"Is that why you got fired?"

"No. My boss told me it was because business has been so slow. I guess I was laid off, not fired."

"Your situation is bad, Hank. I'll be blunt with you. You're guilty of grand theft auto. If they convict you of the pharmacy robbery, that will be two crimes. And the assault on Mr. Warren might be prosecuted as a separate crime. I don't know how the 'three strikes and you're out' rule works, but you might just be facing life in prison. And if Mr. Warren doesn't come out of his coma …"

Hank was trying to stifle his tears, but at this point he began sobbing uncontrollably.

Amarel walked around the table and put her arms around Hank's neck and held him.

"It's okay, Hank, I believe you are innocent. I was questioning it for a while, but I believe you. I'm going to do everything I can to find some proof that you are innocent."

Hank tried to speak between sobs. "Aren't they supposed to prove I'm guilty? It's 'innocent until proven guilty,' isn't it?"

Amarel grabbed a box of tissues from above the refrigerator and set them on the table. Then she sat down in the chair next to Hank, keeping one hand on his shoulder for a moment. "It's supposed to be, but I think they've got enough now that you need to be concerned. Did anyone you know see you jogging that night?"

"Nobody I know. I passed a couple of people, but they'd have no way of knowing that I was jogging rather than running from a crime scene."

"What about the money?"

"They can check my apartment. There's no money there."

"You know the woods pretty well. You could easily have hidden the money in a tree stump to retrieve it later. Can you think of anyone else you know that could have robbed the pharmacy?"

"Well, the ski mask might be a clue. The general public would not have known they were there in the stockroom. It could have been another employee or maybe a delivery truck driver."

"I'm going out for the afternoon," said Amarel. "I'm going to try to find some exculpatory evidence."

"Some what evidence?"

"Exculpatory. It means proving that you are innocent."

"I don't have a prayer, do I?"

"You always have a prayer," said Amarel. "Even if you don't have anything else, you always have a prayer."

CHAPTER 12

HIGH TECH

On the southwest corner of Creekside, there are a few upscale houses where the rich folks of the town live—the president of the bank, the owner of the shirt factory, some of the businessmen. One of the largest and nicest houses in town had just been purchased recently by a young couple who had moved to Creekside from the Silicon Valley. They were barely in their thirties, but they had made a fortune in the programming industry and had retired to Creekside. Amarel had an idea—one of the crazy ideas that she was famous for.

That afternoon, Amarel went calling. She rang the doorbell, which chimed two tones. The place was a little intimidating. The house was huge, at least by Creekside standards. It was a neoclassical home, the kind with pillars supporting the porch roof. The lawn and garden were immaculately cared for. Amarel expected to see Jeeves the butler in a tuxedo answering the door. Instead she was greeted by a sight that put her very much at ease.

"How may I help you?" The man who answered the door was dressed in blue jeans and a sweatshirt with white socks and no shoes. He had an impish smile on his face and a cup of coffee in his hand.

"Are you the computer genius?"

"Ha ha! My wife is the head nerd. I'm just the assistant. "

"Well then, maybe I want to talk to both of you. I have a business proposition."

"Come on in. Have a seat." He pointed her to an overstuffed chair that looked so comfortable that she wasn't sure she'd ever be able to get out of it. Her host stretched out on the couch with his feet up.

"Would you like a cup of coffee?" the man asked.

"No thank you," said Amarel.

"Tea?" This voice came from a lady, presumably the head nerd, who had quietly entered the room while Amarel wasn't looking. She was dressed in tight slacks and a big, bulky sweater with a random earth-tone pattern. She resembled a caterpillar in a cocoon. In fact, she looked a bit like the picture on the sign at The Bookworm. Amarel thought that was pretty cool. She smiled approvingly.

"Do you by any chance have some hot chocolate mix?" said Amarel. It was a chilly, dreary day, the kind when a cup of cocoa is just the perfect thing. Maybe she should not have asked, though. She was imposing on this lovely couple.

"I think we do," said the hostess, "and that sounds good to me as well." She stepped into the kitchen. If the day was chilly for Amarel, it must have felt frigid for these Silicon Valley transplants.

The man then asked, "May I know your name?"

"Amarel."

"Like the Little Mermaid?"

"No, that was Ariel."

"Well, I'm Jim Duncan." He motioned to his wife, who was returning from the kitchen. "This is my wife, Tanya."

"Tanya, this is Amarel, not to be confused with Ariel the mermaid."

"I'm pleased to meet you," said Tanya.

"Amarel was about to propose a business venture," said Jim.

"Perhaps 'business venture' is too elegant a term for it," said Amarel. "I have a problem that requires a genius to solve. It involves facial recognition without a face."

"Ha ha," said Jim. "And how much would we be paid for this gig?"

"Practically nothing."

"Ha ha ha ha." Jim had a charming laugh. If he could change his "Ha ha" to "Ho ho," he would make a great Santa Claus.

"Okay, let me make sure I've got this straight. You want us to solve an impossible problem, and you're going to pay us peanuts. I do hope our lives will be in danger, just to make it interesting."

"I'm sorry," said Amarel. Tears were forming in her eyes. "I guess I hadn't thought through how stupid this all sounds. It's just … I was desperate, and—"

"Hold on," said Jim. "I didn't say we wouldn't do it. As you can probably tell, we're not hurting for money, and we have plenty of time on our hands between performances of the ballet and the symphony." This was a subtle joke. Creekside had no entertainment more sophisticated than the movie theater, and even there, the movies were weeks behind the big city theaters.

"Okay," said Jim. "Lay it out for us. What's the problem?"

"I know that they can use facial recognition to spot terrorists at the airport. I'm hoping we can come up with a way to determine who committed a certain crime. There is a surveillance tape, but the criminal is wearing a ski mask."

Tanya chimed in. "Well, this actually sounds like fun. I know a guy who has worked with facial recognition. He can probably give us some algorithms."

"What is an algorithm?" Amarel asked.

Jim responded, "In geek-speak, it's a method or process for solving a problem. We'd have to adapt it, of course, but it would give us a starting place."

"Then you'll do it?"

He turned to Mrs. Duncan. "What do you think, hun?"

Tanya nodded.

Jim said, "It looks like you've hired yourself a nerd squad. We can't make any promises, but we can certainly take a look at the tape and give it a try."

Amarel picked up the plastic bag she had been carrying and pulled out a DVD. "This is the surveillance video that they showed on TV."

Then she pulled out some yearbooks from the local high school.

"I don't know if this will help, but there are pictures in here of a bunch of people of about the right age. There is also a possibility that the thief was a delivery truck driver who made deliveries to the pharmacy. There is a second file on the disk. It's a picture of the guy they suspect. It was taken with a cell phone, and it's not very clear."

"How soon do you want the results?" asked Jim.

"How soon can you have them?"

"Ha ha ha. I have no idea. I don't know why I even asked that. We'll call when we get something. Oh, which reminds me: do you have a phone number?"

Amarel pulled her cell phone from her purse and opened it. "New cell phone. I haven't memorized the number yet." She found the number and gave it to Jim.

Jim gave her a nicely engraved business card with his phone number. "Okay. We'll call when we get something. Or when we're sure we can't get anything."

CHAPTER 13

THE OTHER END OF TOWN

Amarel worked that evening. When she got home, she told Hank about her plan and about the nerd squad. She asked Hank for more information.

"Do you have any idea who the crook is?"

"I've been thinking about that," said Hank. "The only person who would be likely to know where those ski masks were is Jack Powell. I know I said some of the truck drivers might know, but I really doubt that they would have noticed."

"Is this Jack Powell a shady character?"

"Not particularly, but there is one thing I've noticed. He has called in sick several times on Mondays."

"People get sick on Mondays," said Amarel.

"Yes, but I remember hearing somewhere that that can be a signal of drug use. I know he drinks a lot too, so maybe he's hungover on Mondays."

"How long have you known this guy?"

"He was in my chemistry class in high school. It was supposed to be a senior class, but I talked the school into letting me take it in my junior year."

"So you're an aspiring chemist."

"I really enjoyed chemistry class. I thought that if I ever got to go to college, I'd like to become a chemist."

"Did you know that that's what they call pharmacists in England?"

"Yeah, I've heard that. One of the things I enjoy about working at the pharmacy … that I did enjoy about working at the pharmacy … is handling the chemicals. I always think to myself, 'I'm stocking the acetylsalicylic acid now.'"

Amarel chuckled. "What's that?"

"Aspirin. I just like saying the long names."

"So chemistry was your favorite subject?"

"Yeah, probably. I liked American history, too. Chemistry wins because a lot of it was hands-on, while history was more lecture. I have a short attention span when it comes to lectures. I guess I'm sorta hyperactive."

Amarel said, "I enjoyed English class. I guess you can tell that I like to read a lot."

"Yeah, I noticed that. Do you work as a nurse?"

"No. What made you think that?"

"The way you set everything out so neatly in the bathroom last night. It looked like the way a surgical nurse might arrange things."

"No," said Amarel. "I just have to do things in an orderly way. It keeps me from forgetting things, which I am prone to do otherwise."

"So what do you do?"

"I'm a store clerk. I majored in small business in college. I thought maybe I'd run my own business someday."

"Well, I bet you'd be great at it."

"Thanks. Well, back to work. I'll let my detectives know that they should take a look at Jack Powell. Any other suspects that you can think of?"

"No, not really."

"Do you have any idea where Jack hangs out?"

"At Danny Boy's."

"One more thing: do you know how much money might have been stolen?

"For that drop, my best guess would be around twelve hundred."

Amarel put in a call to her computer geniuses to tell them to check on a Jack Powell.

CHAPTER 14

BUY YOU A DRINK?

THE NEXT MORNING AT THE BREAKFAST TABLE, Amarel continued her questioning of Hank. She had to find out more about Jack Powell. She wanted to know whether he was a likely suspect or whether that was just wishful thinking on Hank's part.

"Any idea how I could get Jack into a conversation?"

"Yeah. Go to Danny Boy's and let him buy you a beer. If you can get him drunk, he'll tell you anything you want to hear. Probably a lot that you don't want to hear, too."

"Would wine work as well as beer?"

"Probably. Yeah, sure."

Amarel was not a drinker. And this was not the time to start. She'd be drunk long before he was.

She concocted a plan. It was midmorning. She didn't know what time Danny Boy's opened, but she figured it would probably be open by noon, so she drove down there. The place was open, but it had very few customers so far.

Amarel walked in, feeling very much out of place in this alien world. She walked up to the bar and sat down. The bartender approached. "What can I get you?"

"Nothing right now, thanks. Just some information. Do you work evenings also?"

"Yeah, sometimes. I'm on tonight."

"Listen, some friends and I are planning an elaborate practical joke. I'm wondering if you would be willing to help out."

"What would I have to do?"

"I'm coming in tonight. I'll order 'my usual' and you'll give me grape juice in a wine glass. I've got the juice in my car. I'll bring it in. That is, if you'll go along."

"Who's the mark?"

"A guy named Jack Powell. Do you know him?"

"Oh yeah. Cool. That guy can be a pain in the butt. I'm in."

"Now I just have to figure out how to get his attention."

"I can help you with that too. I know exactly which buttons to press."

Amarel went to the car and came back in with a large bottle of grape juice.

"Now you're going to remember me, right? You'll remember what I look like?"

"Definitely. Good luck with your prank."

"You'll get a big tip."

Amarel worked at the store that afternoon. She was fortunate to have a boss who didn't mind if the employees exchanged hours, and even luckier to have a coworker who was glad to make such exchanges. That week, her schedule was going absolutely crazy. And she couldn't even tell her coworkers why.

By eight that evening, Amarel was sitting at a table in the bar. The bartender asked if she wanted anything to drink. She hesitated, wondering if he remembered her.

"You beat Jack here. Sometimes he doesn't get here until nine, so you might have a bit of a wait. Would you like your usual while you're waiting?" He winked.

"Sure. Thanks."

"How about some nachos to go with that?"

Until then she hadn't thought about it, but she had not had any supper and suddenly felt famished. "Yes, that would be nice."

"Nachos and a red wine coming up." He made quotation marks in the air as he said "red wine."

Just before nine o'clock, Jack came in.

"Hey Danny Boy, what's cooking," he said in a loud voice. The bartender's name was not Danny, and he looked like he was trying not to appear irritated.

"You want the usual?"

"Yeah. Make it a double."

The waiter waved at Amarel.

Jack looked over his shoulder to see who he was waving at.

"You know that girl?"

"I know that fine lady," said the bartender.

"What's her story?"

"Her story is that she's way out of your league. You'd better just forget it."

"We'll see about that," said Jack. Amarel quickly realized that this was the button that the bartender had promised to press.

Jack walked over to Amarel's table. "Buy ya a drink, little lady?" He may have been trying to sound like John Wayne, but he just wasn't that good of an actor.

Amarel tried to look nonchalant. She paused a moment. "Yeah, sure." Then she called to the bartender. "Kenny, another one please."

Jack sat down. "I haven't seen you here before. I would have remembered."

"I guess you were just unlucky. We've been here different times."

"Maybe tonight I'll get lucky."

Amarel found his sexual innuendo to be neither clever nor appealing as she smiled broadly. "Maybe," she said.

Kenny brought Amarel's usual, winking as he set it down. He also put a drink in front of Jack. It was something on the rocks, but beyond that, Amarel had no idea what it was. He also set a new batch of nachos and a pitcher of beer on the table. Jack handed Kenny two twenties and said to him, "Keep track. We'll be having a couple more." Kenny returned to the bar.

Amarel noticed that the twenties came from a pocket that looked rather stuffed. "By the way," she said to Jack, "can you change a twenty for me?" She didn't need change for a twenty, but she wanted to get a look at the roll of bills, if that was indeed what was in his pocket. Sure enough, he pulled out a big handful of bills. Shuffling through it, he went past a number of twenties and then came to some fives. He handed her four fives, and she handed him a twenty. The fives were brand-new.

"That's quite a stash there," she said. "Are you a doctor?"

"Nah. But there are many ways to make money, if you know what I mean." He winked at her. He acted as though he were propositioning a prostitute.

How disgusting, she thought as she smiled broadly. Then she said, "Many ways to spend it too."

He leaned in close, breathing fermented grain in her face. She kept cool and continued to smile. "The alley right beside the bar is one place you can spend your money."

"Grass?" she said. She had a mild panic, wondering whether she had used the right terminology. Marijuana had been called Mary Jane, pot, broccoli, giggle weed, and a hundred other things. She didn't know if "grass" was the proper term for this place and time. But he didn't seem to react at all.

"Yeah. Good stuff, too."

She had the information she had come for. He had a lot of money—more than he could have gotten legitimately—and he was a drug user. She knew she ought to leave now. She had a strong urge to do so. But she forced herself to stay. She held on to the hope that maybe, just maybe, he would make a flat-out admission of his crime if she got him drunk enough.

Well, the plan did not work. Though he got more drunk, he did not get more honest. He got more obnoxious, louder, and less coherent. He also demonstrated a remarkable capacity to amuse himself. He had one joke that he told over and over. Each time it became less coherent. But each time, he found it even more amusing. On the first telling, he chuckled, and so did she. By the third telling, he was laughing, and she was trying to laugh as well. By the fifth telling, the joke was pretty much incomprehensible and he was guffawing. Amarel tried to pretend she was getting drunk too. But at some point, she realized that he was probably seeing three of her and could not tell which one, if any, was drunk, so she dropped the act.

It was near midnight when she decided to get out of there. Jack asked her, "Do you want to come back to my place?"

Coyly, she replied, "I have to work tomorrow. Do you ever come in here on Fridays?"

"Yeah, sometimes"

"Maybe you can try to catch me on a Friday."

When she got home, she greeted Hank and told him about the money and the drug tip.

Then she said, "Do you need to use the bathroom? I'm going to be in there for a while. I'm going to take a shower. When I'm done, I'm going to take another one.

"That bad, huh?"

She felt as though the disgust of the evening was clinging to her like cigarette smoke clings to leather, and she wanted to try to scrub it off.

CHAPTER 15

GEEK SPEAK

THE NEXT MORNING, Amarel went to see her troop of geniuses. Jim ushered her to the comfortable chair and then called to Tanya. "Hey, hon, Amarel is here."

As they waited for Tanya to arrive, Amarel asked, "Why did you guys move out here to the sticks, anyway? "

"Well," said Jim, "for one thing, we wanted to be able to take a stroll in the evening without being afraid. We like the slower pace. It's a nice change." Then he laughed and added, "Besides, nobody in California walks up to your door and asks you to take on a crazy challenge. You certainly have made life interesting. "

When Tanya arrived, Amarel got down to business. "What have you found out?"

"Well, even with the ski mask we can determine some facial features in a general way," said Jim. "We have about eighty percent accuracy of the robber's facial structure."

"Go on," said Amarel.

"Hank matches that structure at about an eighty percent level."

"Wait. How did you know his name was Hank? I didn't tell you that."

Tanya then chimed in. "We watch the news, and it's a small town.

Anyway, we found Hank's picture in the yearbook and did a test run. Hank doesn't appear as a senior—"

"He dropped out," said Amarel.

"But," said Tanya, "there was a pretty good picture from his junior year. And the program said it was an eighty percent match to the robber."

"Okay, so eighty percent and eighty percent. That sounds like a good match. Do you think he's the one?"

"Not such a good match," said Jim. "Eighty percent of eighty percent is sixty-four percent. That's not a passing grade in most schools. And in a court of law, you need to be beyond a reasonable doubt. You wouldn't want to hang your case on a computer match unless it was like ninety-five percent. Even then, you'd want some corroborating evidence."

"So the tape doesn't prove his guilt. Does it prove his innocence?"

"No," said Jim. "So far, we do not have any proof of anything, one way or the other."

"What about Jack?"

"He's a better match, actually, but still not high enough for a legal case," said Jim.

Then Tanya spoke. "There's something else we wanted to ask you about. I notice that the robber is wearing a high school letter jacket. Was your boyfriend an athlete?"

"Hank is not my boyfriend. Just a friend. He was sort of an athlete. He was on the wrestling team, but second string. He never actually got to compete."

"Whoa!" said Jim, as though some piece of the puzzle had suddenly fallen into place. "Come here."

He went over to his computer and booted it. When it came up, he played the surveillance tape.

"This is not Hank," said Jim.

"How do you know?"

"Wrestlers are trained on how to wrestle. It's more than just physical skills. They learn an attitude too. They're always alert. They have a way of standing; a way of walking. This is not a wrestler's walk. It's more of a drunken sailor walk."

"So if it's not Hank, who is it?"

"The walk isn't going to help us much when all we have to compare to is still photos," said Jim.

"Okay. Thanks for trying. I guess I owe you a bag of peanuts for your effort."

"Well, we're not done yet," said Jim. "We're idea people, and you never know when a brilliant idea will hit."

"Or *if* one will," said Amarel.

"That's true. But we're not giving up yet. Don't you give up, either."

Amarel made another stop on her way home. She went back to Danny Boy's. She hoped that Kenny would be on duty. He was.

"Hi, Kenny. Thanks for your help last night. I owe you some money."

"Jack paid for your drinks and nachos."

"No, I mean I promised you a big tip." She pulled a twenty from her wallet.

"You don't have to do that."

"I promised you a big tip, and I keep my promises. Besides, you have to put up with that jerk. You deserve some compensation."

"Well thank you. Come back again. The next batch of nachos is on the house."

Work was difficult that evening. Amarel was too preoccupied. It seemed that the mystery was solved, but not in a way that would hold up in court. And as far as the police knew, Hank was still the guilty party.

CHAPTER 16

TROUBLE

THE NEXT MORNING, Amarel happened to glance out her back window. Something was wrong. She had put the bag containing Hank's discarded clothes in the alley for the trash pickup. This was not trash day, and the bag was gone. Hank came into the kitchen and sat down at the table.

"Good morning, Amy. How are you today?"

She didn't answer. She was obviously distracted. She kept staring out the back window. After a while, she said, "Did you see anything unusual in the alley behind the house?"

"No, why? Is something wrong?" asked Hank.

She thought for a moment. "No, probably not." She said this without much conviction. She couldn't figure out any logical reason that the bag would not be there. But then neither could she figure out any reason that anyone would steal her trash. *Must have got washed away in the big flood.*

She made egg sandwiches for herself and Hank. When she placed Hank's sandwich in front of him, he said, "Thanks for the food."

Amarel said, "You're welcome."

"No, that was a prayer. Did I get it right?"

"Perfect!"

As they ate, Hank asked some questions that had been spurred by the book he had read. Some were simple factual questions: where is Nazareth? That sort of thing. Then he hit her with a big one.

"Is God one person or three?"

"He's three in one. That's the concept of the Trinity."

"That doesn't make any sense to me at all. Even if we were just talking about two people, separate people have separate personalities, separate experiences, separate thoughts. In what sense could they be one person?"

"It's a mystery. We can't expect to understand it completely with our feeble minds."

"I thought you had all the answers."

"No, not by a long shot. I know just as much as I need to know to take the next step in my life's journey, but not much more. Sometimes even the next step is not very clear, but God leads me."

"That's not a very helpful answer."

"Here's one way to think of it. You know, sometimes a husband and wife get to know each other so well that they can finish each other's ..." She drew out the word "others" so as to give Hank a chance to finish it. "Finish each other's ..."

"Sandwiches. No, sentences."

Amarel laughed. Hank had used a very old joke that he had seen on TV. But Amarel didn't watch much TV, so the joke was new to her. And it struck her right on the funny bone. She laughed hard. Hank started laughing too. He was more amused by her response than by the joke itself, but Amarel's laughter was contagious. She laughed so hard that she was in tears and gasping for breath.

"Thank you, Hank. I needed a good laugh."

"I guess I should thank you, too," said Hank. "You really got me going too."

"Anyway," said Amarel, "the Father, Son, and Spirit finish each other's sandwiches. And sentences. Not a solidly theological explanation, I know, but it's one way of thinking about the trinity."

She looked away for a moment and then said, "There's something else I need."

"What's that?"

"Some quiet time. I'm going to my sanctuary for a while."

"You mean the place in the woods?" asked Hank.

"Yes."

"Are you closer to God there?"

"No. Wherever I go, God is there with me. My sanctuary isn't closer to God, but it feels like it sometimes. Probably because it's quiet there."

"It's not so quiet," said Hank. "Try sleeping there sometime. Lots of noisy birds and bugs."

"Just the heavens declaring the glory of God."

CHAPTER 17

DEEP TROUBLE

AMAREL WENT OUT TO HER SANCTUARY. Today she was struck by the cathedral-like appearance of her little grass plot. Big trees formed a Gothic arch overhead while some younger trees played the role of flying buttresses. There was an isolated tree at the uphill end of the grass plot. If you looked at it just right, you could see a crucifix in it.

Although the setting seemed more perfect than ever for spiritual refreshment, the refreshment just would not come. Instead Amarel had a vague feeling of foreboding, as though danger lay ahead. She had a prayer list that she kept in her head, but this time she could not read it. She did pray for Hank, though. She spoke softly. "Father, let him understand your redeeming love. But how can he understand a father's redeeming love for one of his children? His earthly father has not been much of an example."

And she prayed for herself. "'Wisdom' and 'courage.' Why do those two words keep popping into my mind? Peace is what I want to pray for. Please. I want this sense of foreboding to go away. Peace. Please." But peace didn't come. "Not my will, but thine be done." Inexplicably, when she spoke those words, a sense of peace did at last come to her.

She whispered one last prayer: a prayer of thanks for Susie. They had again traded shifts.

She went to work, and the afternoon went smoothly. She was a bit tired by the time she got home. She was heading for her front door when her dear neighbor Sally Reynolds came out to her porch. "Amy, dear."

Sally was a senior citizen, and not very spry, so Amarel walked over to her porch. Sally was a woman of wisdom, and Amarel enjoyed hearing her stories. She often went over to Sally's house just to chat, and sometimes to help with some little task: changing a bulb in the ceiling light—that sort of thing. Sally also played a mean game of Scrabble, and Amarel enjoyed the challenge.

"Amy dear, are you in some kind of trouble?"

"Why do you ask?"

"The police were stopped behind your house early this morning."

Did they take the trash bag? I tied it initially. I untied it to take the jacket and remove the wrestling letter. Did I retie it? I bet I didn't. Someone must have seen the jacket and called them. That's the only explanation that makes any sense.

"Did you see anything else?" Amarel asked. "Could you see what they were doing there?"

"I couldn't see what they were doing, but they were there for several minutes. Amy dear, are you in trouble?"

"Yes, Mrs. Reynolds, I think maybe I am."

"Is there anything I can do for you?"

"I wish there was. I think I've made a real mess of things."

"Would some money help?" asked Sally.

A plan was hatching in Amarel's mind, another one of her crazy plans—but this one would be costly. "No, Mrs. Reynolds. I can't take your money. You need it. Besides, it would take a lot of money."

"You stay right there, dear."

She went into the house and reemerged in a minute or so with a stack of bills. "Here, dear, that's about two hundred dollars."

"Mrs. Reynolds, I can't ask you for this."

"You didn't ask. I gave. If our positions were reversed, you wouldn't even stop to think about it. You'd give me the shirt off your back. You know you would. Now then, you go to Redeemer Community Church, don't you?"

"Yes," said Amarel.

"You know Richard and Lisa Evans, don't you?"

"Yes."

"You go on over to their house," said Sally. "Go on, hurry."

Amarel walked on over to the Evanses' house. But she didn't hurry. She was trying to figure out what to say to them. She knew she shouldn't tell them her plan. It was just too crazy. And if things went awry, she didn't want anyone other than herself to bear any blame.

Before she could figure out what to say, Mr. Evans met her at the door.

"Here you go, Amy." He handed her a fistful of money. "Tommy Diaz's place is your next stop. Do you know where that is?"

She knew. She started walking toward the Diaz home. By the time she got there, she was going something between a speed walk and a run.

She received the same greeting and response at the Diaz house.

At the Elliot place, she was given a handful of money that had been stuffed into a travel pouch, the kind travelers use for toiletries. That was helpful, as the stack of cash was getting quite big.

From the Elliots', she went to the Everetts', and then the Martins'. There Mr. Martin said, "Your next stop is—"

"Wait," Amarel said, interrupting. "This is my last stop. I've got what I need. Please thank them for being willing to donate for me. I won't be able to do it personally. Thank you so much. God bless you!"

She actually didn't have quite what she needed. She was about a hundred short, but she had a hundred stashed in a secret place at home. She figured that she should be among the investors in this crazy scheme.

At home, she worked quickly. She pulled a book off of her shelf and opened it. The book had been hollowed out to make a compartment where she kept some cash. She added it to the rest. She also added the cash from her purse.

She sat down next to Hank and handed him her cell phone. "Here, Hank. This is my cell phone. Keep it close, and answer it when it rings. Stay inside until you hear otherwise." She looked him square in the eyes. "Do you trust me?"

"You're the only one I trust."

"Then trust me when I tell you this: Don't be afraid. Everything is going to be all right."

"What's going on?"

"I'll tell you later." As she said this, she was already walking toward the door.

CHAPTER 18

BOOK 'EM

AMAREL WALKED OVER TO THE POLICE STATION. She would have run, but she was still a bit out of breath.

She walked into the office. Looking around, she saw that the service desk to the left of the door was unmanned. One wall was lined with file cabinets. At the back of the room was a hallway. She could just barely see some iron bars on one side of the hallway. There were two desks; the back one was empty. At the front desk sat a slender, fit, uniformed officer. The small radio on his desk was playing easy-listening music. The officer seemed intent on dealing with the clutter of file folders on his desk. He barely stopped to look at Amarel but gestured for her to take the empty chair next to his desk.

Without looking up, he asked, "How may I help you?"

"Have you solved the pharmacy robbery case yet?"

The officer raised his eyes and gave Amarel his full attention. "We've got some leads. Why?"

"I understand you found some clothes."

"What do you know about the clothes?"

"I know where you found them."

He glanced at a piece of paper clipped to the front of one of his file folders and then asked, "Are you Amarel Richcreek?" He put the emphasis on the second syllable.

"Amarel," she said, putting the accent on the third syllable. Then she pulled a stack of cash from the travel pouch. "I think you'll find that this is the amount taken from the pharmacy, give or take a few bucks."

"Is there something you'd like to tell us about this money?"

"No," said Amarel. "I don't want to tell you anything until I talk to a lawyer."

"If you're going to lawyer up, I'll need to lock you in the tomb."

"What?"

"I'll need to put you in the holding cell. We call it the tomb."

"That's fine," said Amarel.

He led her into the hallway. The holding cell door opened onto the hallway. It was small and dimly lit. There was an enclosure in one corner containing a toilet and sink.

The officer asked, "Do you have a lawyer, or should I call a public defender?"

"I don't have a lawyer."

"Okay. I'll call the public defender's office. It's going to take a while. Do you want a Pepsi or something?"

"Some cold water, please, if you have any."

"Coming right up." said the officer. "By the way, my name is Officer Nelson."

He walked away and soon returned with a cold bottle of water.

Then he asked her, "Are you hungry? Do you want something to eat?"

She realized then that she hadn't eaten since breakfast. She thought it odd that it hadn't even occurred to her to be hungry. But now she realized that her stomach was empty.

"No thank you," she said.

She had started a fast. It was unintentional, but she guessed that it would still count.

CHAPTER 19

COUNSEL

AMAREL WAS IN THE HOLDING CELL for over an hour before the public defender showed up to talk to her. He asked Officer Nelson if there was a place where he could sit down with his client in private. They were led into what must have been a lunchroom, among other things. It had a small refrigerator in one corner, with a microwave oven sitting on top of it. Next to that was a counter. The opposite side of the room had a stack of boxes of printer paper and a shelf full of other office supplies. In the center of the room was a small table with four folding chairs. The lawyer sat down and gestured for Amarel to sit across from him. The lawyer introduced himself as George Snyder from the public defender's office.

"Call if you need anything," said Officer Nelson as he closed the door.

Amarel had been thinking through her options. She could plead guilty, but that would be a lie. She would be bearing false witness, but it would be against herself, not her neighbor. *Does that count?* She wondered. Honesty was important to her. She could not plead guilty.

Amarel spoke first. "I know that there is a way to plead that is neither a guilty plea nor a not guilty plea."

The attorney said, "You're getting way ahead of yourself. You won't be asked for a plea until arraignment. That's several steps down the road."

Amarel said, "Would you answer my question please?"

"There is a nolo contendere plea, but it is usually only used as part of a plea bargain. It's occasionally used by a politician to avoid jail time. It's definitely not an appropriate plea in this case."

"My plea will be nolo contendere."

"But that plea just isn't used under normal circumstances, and there's nothing extraordinary about your case. I talked to the officer earlier. He tells me that you are a suspect in a robbery. He also suggested that the evidence is weak. My recommendation is that you plead not guilty. It looks to me like we can get you off easily. That's if they even file charges. I don't think the officer even believes that you are guilty."

She again said, "My plea will be nolo contendere."

"Are you guilty?"

"I don't want to say."

"Are you insane? Because you're acting crazy."

"I know what I'm doing."

"Well I don't. Do you want to explain it to me?"

"No, I'm sorry, I don't."

Amarel and the lawyer conversed for about half an hour. Actually, "conversation" might not be the best term to describe their meeting. The lawyer did most of the talking. Amarel said nothing of consequence.

Finally the lawyer exited the room and closed the door behind him, but Amarel could hear him speaking to Officer Nelson outside.

"Guilty or not guilty?" asked Officer Nelson.

The lawyer shook his head and sighed. "If you file charges, her plea will be nolo contendere."

"Are you sure that's a good idea?"

"I'm sure it's a bad idea, but she is within her rights, and that's what she wants to do."

"Well then, I don't see that I have any choice but to book her. Counselor, come with me."

The door opened, and Officer Nelson looked directly at Amarel.

"Amarel Joanne Richcreek, you are under arrest. You have the right to remain silent. If you give up the right to remain silent"— George nodded at Amarel, suggesting that he wanted her to give up her right to remain silent, but she didn't—"anything you say can and will be used against you in a court of law. You have the right to counsel. If you cannot afford counsel, a lawyer will be appointed for you. You have a right to have counsel with you during questioning. Do you understand these rights?"

"Yes I do," said Amarel.

"With these rights in mind, are you willing to give us a statement at this time?"

George jumped in. "It would be a very good idea for you to make a statement, Miss Richcreek."

"I do not wish to make a statement," said Amarel.

Officer Nelson said, "I have to put you back in the tomb."

"Do I get one phone call?"

"You watch too much TV. You can have as many local calls as you need." This amused Amarel slightly, for she seldom watched TV, and never police shows.

There was a phone in the lunchroom. Officer Nelson told her to let him know when she was finished. She dialed her own cell phone number.

"Hello?"

"Hi, Hank. It's Amy."

"What's up?"

"It's okay for you to go outside if you want now. The police are not looking for you. They have someone in custody."

"They got Jack?"

"No. Someone else."

"I don't understand. What's going on?"

Amarel was silent.

"Amy, what's going on?"

"Redemption."

CHAPTER 20

PROCESSING

Officer Nelson filled out some paperwork for Amarel. Under "aliases," the name Amy was listed. He had checked the computerized database while she was talking to her lawyer. He was surprised to find nothing on file, not even a speeding ticket. Nevertheless, he determined that she had to be handcuffed. That was standard procedure for a violent offense. Her attorney tried to convince Officer Nelson that this was unnecessary, but Amarel said that procedures should be followed and that she did not want any special treatment.

The lawyer said, "I will meet you at county, and we'll have you out on bail, probably within an hour."

"I am not applying for bail," said Amarel.

The lawyer was becoming very distraught, and Amarel noticed. "Hey, George, cheer up. You're doing a great job. I'll be glad to give you a good recommendation anytime you need one."

"Thanks. A letter of recommendation for a defense attorney coming from a state prison cell is just what my career needs." He turned to the policeman while pulling a business card from his pocket. "Officer, here's my number. If Miss Richcreek changes her mind, you'll know how to reach me. In fact, let me write my cell phone number on the back. Call me anytime." He scrawled the number on the back of the card and handed it to Officer Nelson. Then he left.

Officer Nelson loaded Amarel into the back of the police car. After she had buckled her seat belt, he cuffed her wrists again.

Amarel felt that the drive to county would never end. She was weak from not eating all day.

Upon arriving at county, Amarel was informed that she was being "processed." It sounded to her like something they do to chicken parts on an assembly line. She soon realized that that was just how it felt, too. At the first station, she was told to empty her pockets and remove any jewelry. An officer listed every item that was presented.

She was led to a second station where she was told to stand near a wall that was marked with horizontal lines one foot apart. There were inch marks in between. "Turn right." A flash went off. "Straight ahead." Another flash. "Turn left." A third flash. Amarel noticed that the photographer had not asked her to smile. The officer made notes of her hair color, complexion, eye color, and distinguishing marks. The officer seemed a bit surprised that she had no tattoos.

At the third station, an officer grabbed her right hand, pressed her thumb onto an ink pad, and then rolled her thumb on a sheet of paper. This process was repeated with each finger of her right hand, and then her left hand.

She was roughly dragged or pushed from station to station. Then she was ordered into a small changing room where she was told to strip down to her underwear. She was then given a loose-fitting bright orange top and pants with a drawstring and was told to put them on. Her sneakers were checked and found to be metal-free, so she was allowed to put them back on.

Her clothes were added to the earlier inventory list. Everything was placed in a numbered box. She was told to sign the inventory if it was correct. It was, and she did.

Finally, she was passed off to a uniformed female guard, who led her down a hallway to a steel-barred gate, which slid open slowly. The guard escorted her through. All of the guards up to this point had seemed to treat her with distain, but this one was a bit gentler.

Amarel heard the steel gate clang shut behind her. She wasn't ready for what that would sound like, and for the briefest moment, she wondered if she had been shot. She gasped. Up to that point, she had been doing well, but now a sense of terror grabbed hold of her. A second steel gate opened and closed; then a third. The clang of the closing gates seemed to echo forever.

Between the third and fourth gate was a hallway. Halfway down the hallway, the guard stopped. "Have you ever been in prison before, honey?"

"No."

"I didn't think so. Let me give you a nickel's worth of free advice. Keep to yourself. Don't try to start any conversations. And don't look anyone straight in the eye." That last part would be a problem. Amarel routinely looked people in the eye. She was a good judge of people, and a straight look was the technique that she used.

Then they resumed their walk. The fourth door opened and closed. Beyond it was a set of cells—cages, really—six in number. The guard removed Amarel's handcuffs and opened the second cell door on the left side with a key.

"Ooh, looky here," said an inmate. "They done brought us a debutante! What's ya doin' here, Miss Debutante?"

"Leave her alone," said the guard. She closed the cell door and walked away. She headed for the guard station, where two other guards were already seated. The three sat there, one solving a Sudoku, the others chatting about nothing in particular. Ten minutes later, they heard a bloodcurdling scream. All three of them ran to cell two.

"Back off, Tiffany!" said one of the guards as she opened the cell door. The other two rushed toward Tiffany and in a flash had her facedown on the floor. One of them grabbed an object from her hand and tossed it out of the cell. In seconds Tiffany was cuffed and was being led away by one of the guards. Meanwhile, the guard with the key was kneeling beside Amarel, who was on the floor, leaning against the steel bars and moaning. She was covered with blood. The guard grabbed a pillow from one of the cots, removed the pillowcase, and wrapped it around Amarel's right hand, which seemed to be the source of most of the blood. She was quivering, and the guard had trouble wrapping her hand.

"Hold that in place, honey. Keep some pressure on it." Amarel recognized the voice as belonging to the guard that had led her to the cell earlier.

In seconds, Amarel and the guard were moving down a hallway. Amarel must have been walking, but she could not sense that her feet were moving. The whole situation seemed unreal, like a nightmare. Things that she looked at were not clear. Part of that was because she was trying to see through her own tears.

They stepped into a white room.

"Lay down there on the table, honey."

Amarel closed her eyes.

CHAPTER 21

AN ANGEL OF MERCY

" ... YOUR NAME? Can you tell me your name?"

"Amy."

"Good girl. Do you know where you are?"

Amarel opened her eyes slowly. The lights were bright and hurt her eyes at first. She looked around. The woman who was speaking to her was wearing a white lab coat. She also saw a sink and a supply cabinet.

"I thought I was in jail," said Amarel, "but this doesn't look like a jail."

"You're in the prison infirmary. Do you know how you got here?"

"I think I walked here. With some help. The last thing I remember is someone telling me to lay down."

"After that, you fainted."

"What time is it?"

"It's about one a.m."

"Are you the doctor?"

"I'm a nurse practitioner. My name is Angela. The lady in the chair there is Cindy Marino. She's the guard who helped you walk here." Amarel looked at the woman sitting in the corner of the room. It was the same guard who had told her earlier to keep to herself.

Amarel lifted her hands and looked at the palms. They were heavily bandaged.

"Those are what we call defensive wounds," said Angela. "One of the other prisoners tried to stab you."

"Tiffany," said Amarel.

"Yes. Her name is Tiffany. She's a little territorial about her cell. Do you remember doing or saying anything to provoke her?"

"I don't think I did anything."

"You probably didn't. She's got a hair trigger. How do the hands feel?"

Her left hand hurt plenty, but it was nothing compared to the right hand, which was feeling waves of throbbing pain. "I've been better," she said.

I'm going to give you a shot for the pain," said Angela. "Do you know when you last had a tetanus shot?"

"No. It's been several years at least."

"Okay. I'm going to give you a tetanus shot as well."

"Do you remember how the fight started?" asked Angela.

"I don't think it was a fight. I remember her … remember Tiffany saying something about how I should stop staring at her. Then I saw her coming at me with something in her hand. I guess I just tried to block with my hands. I guess it was instinctive."

"Okay. The object was a plastic knife from the dining hall. She had rubbed it on the concrete until it was shaped more like an ice pick. It appears that you deflected the knife with your left hand and then it plunged into your right hand. It's a really deep wound. Actually, you're quite lucky. If she had stabbed you in that side of your neck, you would have bled to death before anyone could get to you."

"I don't feel so lucky," said Amarel.

"No, I don't guess that you do. You're still looking pretty pale. What have you had to eat today? Or should I say yesterday?"

"I had an egg sandwich for breakfast."

"Is that it?"

"I'm fasting."

"I think you'll have to stop fasting for a while. Doctor's orders."

"But you're not a doctor," said Amarel.

"Are you going to waste my time getting a doctor to come in here to give you orders?"

"I'll try to eat something."

Cindy stood and walked out the door, saying, "I'll see if I can round up some food."

"You may be a little dehydrated as well," said Angela. "Can you drink some water?"

"That I can do."

Angela pulled a bottle of water from a small refrigerator and handed it to Amarel.

Amarel tried to open it. Angela saw her wincing in pain and said, "You better let me open that for you."

Cindy came back carrying an apple and a pack of snack crackers. Amarel ate the apple first. It was sweet and juicy, and it provided her with the first pleasant sensations she had felt in many hours.

While Amarel ate, Cindy and Angela stepped out of the room and talked. Amarel could hear them, but not well enough to know what they were saying.

Angela soon returned and said, "You are not to be placed back in the general prison population until you have healed. Doctor's orders. Unless you want to object that I'm not a doctor."

Amarel replied by saying, "No objections, Your Honor."

"You look like you've been through a war tonight. I don't care what your crime was; nobody should have to go through something like that."

Cindy had gone away, evidently to figure out what other arrangements could be made. When she returned, she announced that Amarel would be going back to the holding cell in the Creekside police station.

Amarel found that the ride back to her first jail felt like a freeing experience as compared to the previous few hours. She nearly fell asleep multiple times en route, but each time she began to drift off, a wave of pain would wake her. But as soon as she hit the cot in Creekside, she was sleeping soundly. She slept late into the morning.

CHAPTER 22

GENIUSES TO THE RESCUE

Hank had stayed in Amarel's house overnight. Even though she had said he was safe to go out, he just didn't feel safe. In midmorning, Amarel's cell phone rang.

"Hello?"

A male voice replied. "Uh ... I'm sorry. I must have the wrong number."

"Are you calling Amy?"

"I'm calling Amarel."

"Same person. This is her phone."

"Is she there? This is Jim."

"Are you one of the computer guys?"

"Yes, that's me."

"Amy isn't here." Hank paused. "I think she may be in jail."

"What jail?"

"You could ask at the police station."

"We're on our way," said Jim.

"Wait! ... Are you still there?"

"Yes."

"Could you take me with you?" asked Hank.

"Sure. Where are you?"

Hank gave the address and then said, "Would you happen to have a jacket I can borrow? Mine is torn."

"Yeah, sure. We'll see you in a few minutes."

Hank was nervous. He decided to play a game of solitaire while he waited. When he heard the car pull up in front of the house, he scooped up the cards and absentmindedly held them in his hand as he ran to the car. Jim handed him the jacket. He put it on and shoved the cards into the pocket. Then he jumped into the backseat.

Jim took his place at the steering wheel. Turning to Hank he said, "Hank, this is my wife, Tanya. She's the other 'computer guy.'"

Jim started the engine and pulled away from the house. Five minutes later, they were walking into the police station.

Hank immediately asked the officer, "Where's Amy?"

Amy heard the question and recognized Hank's voice. She called out, "Hank?" Hank hurried back along the hallway to the holding cell. The officer initially reached out to stop him, but then let him go.

When Hank saw Amy, he again thought of the poem that had been on his mind lately. "*She walks in beauty like the night of starry something and something something.*" *What happened to that beauty I saw just hours ago?* Amarel was dressed in an ugly prison uniform, looking like a giant, emaciated Halloween pumpkin. Her hands were covered with bandages. Her hair was disheveled, and bits of it were matted with blood. And there was pain in her expression that seemed to surge whenever she moved her right hand.

"What happened to you?" Hank asked.

"Fell off my bicycle," said Amarel.

"Girl, you're even crazier than I thought you were."

Hank heard bits of the conversation at Officer Nelson's desk and walked over to hear better.

Jim was doing the talking. He said, "Amarel is not the robber. We can prove that."

Officer Nelson looked at Hank suspiciously. Hank tensed up.

"It's not Hank either," said Jim.

"Do you know who it is?"

"We think so. We'll lay it all out for you. Does Amy have a lawyer?"

"If he hasn't quit the profession," said Officer Nelson.

"Huh?"

"Amy told him that she would plead nolo contendere. The lawyer had never even seen a nolo contendere case and didn't know what to do with it.

CHAPTER 23

LAYING IT OUT

Amarel said that she wanted her lawyer to be there for the presentation, so everyone—Tanya and Jim, Officer Nelson, Hank, and Amarel—had to sit around and wait while he made the long trip.

They all met in the lunchroom, which was rather crowded. Jim opened his laptop and turned it on. He placed it on the table where everyone would be able to see.

Jim began his presentation. "We know Mrs. Warren. We went to see her and told her we might be able to get some clues if we did a computer analysis of the surveillance tape. She gave us several videos. This still is taken from the video from the night of the robbery. This is the robber passing by the hair-care products. Notice how tall he is compared to the merchandise on the shelf."

He pulled a second picture up on the other half of the screen. "This is a routine tape of a few days earlier. That's Hank by the hair-care shelf. Notice his height, about the same as the robber's."

Hank tensed up as though he were being hunted down. Amarel saw this and touched him on the arm. "Relax, Hank. I think I know where they're going with this."

"Hank and Amy, would you stand back-to-back please?"

They did.

"As you can see, Hank is a good three inches taller than Amy. Since the robber and Hank are about the same height, that means that the robber is a good three inches taller than Amy, too, so Amy cannot be the robber.

"Now just for completeness, we want to show you what didn't work for identification purposes. This is the robber, wearing the ski mask. We ran a structural analysis on the face. This was tricky, since you can't actually see the face. Still, we were able to get an approximation. This would not serve as proof of guilt, but it might be sufficient to prove innocence in some cases. Here's the structure."

He clicked a button, and the masked face was replaced with what appeared to be a bunch of blue Tinkertoys connected to form the general outline of a face.

Jim brought up Hank's picture again. "This is Hank's facial structure. With another key click, Hank's face was replaced with the Tinkertoy model.

"You may be able to see that there is some similarity there. Computer analysis sets the similarity at eighty percent. We also have eighty percent certainty of the shape of the masked face. That means that there is an eighty-percent-times-eighty-percent, or sixty-four percent, match between Hank and the masked man. That is not low enough to establish Hank's innocence. But it is not nearly high enough to establish his guilt, either. Now, to clear Hank."

Amarel saw Hank's ears perk up at the last bit. He was still noticeably nervous.

"Now then, Hank, I understand that you were a wrestler."

"Well, sort of. I was second string. I never actually wrestled in competition."

"Nevertheless, you learned to remain alert like a wrestler. You learned the stance and the walk. Now, this is the tape of the robbery. When the robber comes out of the restroom area, you can see that he takes four walking steps before he starts running. That is not a wrestler's walk. It's what I would call a sailor walk. Sort of a waddle. Now, for comparison, we'll go back to the surveillance tape from the week before. This is Hank walking. You can see the difference. A computer analysis of the two walks rates them as a twenty-four-percent match. That is low enough to constitute good evidence of Hank's innocence."

"Does that mean that we can go home?" asked Amarel.

"No it doesn't," said Officer Nelson. "We still have other evidence against you, Miss Richcreek."

Amarel turned and looked at her lawyer as if to say, "Why didn't you tell me what evidence they had?"

The lawyer asked Officer Nelson to state what other evidence there was.

"The stack of money that Amy brought in included four new five-dollar bills. We know that they came from the pharmacy. We know that the pharmacy put a new pack of fives in the cash register before the robbery. At the end of the day, some of those fives remained in the register. Some had been given out as change during the day, but ordinarily you get only one five-dollar bill in change. Sometimes you might get three, but ordinarily you would never get four. Since Amy had four of the new fives, with consecutive numbers, we assume that she didn't get them as change. They could only have come from the deposit bag that night. The serial numbers prove that they came from that same batch."

Amarel glared at her lawyer. "Why didn't they tell us this? Aren't they supposed to share their evidence with us?"

"Ordinarily, yes, although that wouldn't happen until later in the process. But a plea of nolo contendere means that you do not intend to mount a defense. Therefore, there is no reason for us to have the evidence. And since we are not mounting a defense, the district attorney does not have to mount a vigorous prosecution. They might not even need to mention the five-dollar-bill evidence to get a conviction."

Officer Nelson said to Amarel, "Would you like to tell us where you got that stack of money?"

"Jack Powell gave me change for a twenty. That's where the new fives came from. I borrowed the rest from friends."

"I'm afraid that your word on that is not sufficient," said Officer Nelson. "After all, you're not a disinterested party in this case. You have a reason to tell us that even if it weren't true. I'm afraid you're still a prime suspect. It looks like you didn't do the robbery alone, but you're in possession of stolen cash, and the jacket that was used to break into the garage and steal the ATV was found at your house, so you could still be an accomplice."

"May I continue, officer?" said Jim. "We have some more tape that might interest you."

"Go ahead."

Jim began the second part of his presentation. "Amy mentioned Jack Powell's name, so we decided to check him out. We did the facial recognition and got an eighty-three-percent match. That's a little better than Hank's, but still not sufficient to overcome reasonable doubt." He paused and started another video on his computer. "We managed to secure a video taken at Jack's graduation. Hold on a minute."

They watched several people receive their diplomas and walk off the stage.

"Okay, here comes Jack," said Jim. "He's receiving his diploma. Now watch as he walks the rest of the way across the stage."

"Sailor walk," said Officer Nelson.

"Sailor walk," said Jim. "We ran the computerized comparison of the walks. It was a ninety- to ninety-five-percent match."

"That's not enough to get a conviction," said Officer Nelson.

"Is it enough to get a search warrant?" asked George.

Officer Nelson thought about it for a moment. "I expect so. Let me make a call."

George asked for a moment alone with his client, so everyone else left the lunchroom.

"Amy," he said, "as an officer of the court, I have an obligation to tell you that you could still be prosecuted for giving false evidence. The good news is that the DA has a heavy caseload and isn't looking for more crimes to prosecute. I'll talk to him. I'm pretty sure he won't charge you."

"What about Hank?" asked Amarel. "Will they charge him with car theft?"

"They might. It depends a lot on what the uncle wants to do. I suspect they'll assign me to his case too, so I'll go ahead and make a call to the uncle. Now I have a favor to ask of you."

"What's that?"

"If you ever pull a crazy stunt like this again, do it in a different county."

Amarel laughed. "I'll try to remember that. Thanks, George. You've been terrific. Really."

"All in a day's work," said George, "albeit an unusual day."

They left the lunchroom and went to Officer Nelson's desk. Officer Nelson said, "I'm sorry, Miss Richcreek. No luck yet. Judges don't sit around home on Saturday waiting to issue search warrants. I'll keep trying, but I'm afraid you're stuck in the tomb for now."

"The tomb?" said George.

"The holding cell."

"Can I have visitors?" asked Amarel.

Officer Nelson smiled. "Maybe I can confine you to the break room until evening."

"I'm staying," said Hank.

Jim and Tanya looked at each other and then smiled in perfect sync. Tanya said, "We're staying for a while too, if that's okay."

"Absolutely," said Amarel.

Amarel looked at Hank. "You know, I bet those two finish each other's—"

"Sandwiches. No, sentences." Hank was right on cue.

Everyone chuckled, partly in amusement and partly in relief.

Officer Nelson came back in after just a minute or two. "The prisoner is entitled to be fed. Would you guys like a pizza?"

They assembled an order: pizza, buffalo wings, and beverages. Then Jim reached for his wallet and pulled out some cash. "Here, this one's on us. Our current employer is vastly overpaying us, so it's the least we can do."

"Amarel," said Tanya, "we were hoping that we could get together with you from time to time. We haven't met a whole lot of people in this town yet, and it would be great to have another friend here."

"I think we can work that out," said Amarel, "on one condition."

"What's that?" Tanya asked.

"My friends call me Amy."

The group spent the afternoon devouring pizza and chatting. It ended up being a very nice afternoon, actually, aside from the fact that they were in jail. They shared life stories. Then Hank asked Amarel for the details of how she had ended up there—and the more critical question: why?

"You told me you couldn't go to jail," she said. "I knew that I could."

"But you were nearly killed," Hank replied.

"We talked about that too. Remember? What you said—I think these were your exact words—'If they put me in jail it will kill me.' I was ready to die if I had to. I know where I'm going when I die."

Hank was left speechless.

There was silence for a moment. Then Hank reached into his jacket pocket. "Well, look what we have here." He pulled out his new deck of cards.

"Does everyone know how to play hearts?" Amarel asked.

"I don't," said Hank.

"It's high time you learned. Sit across from me. You'll be my partner."

Hank smiled, obviously pleased with that plan.

After several hours, they decided to heat up the leftover pizza and wings. Between hands, they shared more bits of their life stories. It was a most pleasant afternoon of playing, chatting, and munching, although the fact that they were in jail did take a bit of the shine off of the party.

Around six that evening, Officer Nelson entered the room and announced that he was going off duty. He said, "I'm afraid visiting hours are over. Amy, you'll have to go back to the tomb. You'll have a couple minutes to say your good-byes, and then Officer Fisher will be coming for you."

Jim and Tanya left the room first. Amy then gazed into Hank's eyes for a long moment. Finally she said, "I guess I'll be seeing you." Hank nodded and then left the room.

Officer Fisher soon arrived and escorted Amarel to the holding cell. She walked to her cot and was about to sit down on it, but instead, she knelt on the floor.

Officer Fisher saw her and said, "We have an extra pillow here. That doesn't look very comfortable."

"I don't want to get your pillow dirty."

"Don't worry about that. It will come out in the wash."

"Thank you," said Amarel.

She placed the pillow under her knees. He was right. The concrete floor was not very comfortable. This was much better.

Amarel had not had a quiet prayer session for a long time. She routinely prayed for one person on each of her lists: someone in authority, a friend, an enemy, and an angel. She couldn't remember the next name on any of the lists. Officer Nelson was someone in authority. Tiffany would do nicely for the enemy list. She had so many friends to be thankful for. She prayed in turn for Tanya and Jim, the genius squad; Kenny, the bartender at Danny Boy's; Cindy, the prison matron; and George, the attorney. For the angel list, she thought of the nurse practitioner. Angela the angel: the coincidence of that had escaped her up to that moment. And there were the judges of the county. She didn't know their names or even how many of them there were. She did know that one of them would eventually sign a search warrant. She prayed long and hard for Hank. Her mind kept coming back to Hank. *He's so close,* she thought.

Her body jerked suddenly. She realized that while kneeling there, she had fallen asleep, or nearly so. It was time for her to get into bed.

CHAPTER 24

THE NIGHTMARE ENDS

IT MUST HAVE BEEN ABOUT SIX A.M. The sun was just coming over the horizon. Amarel was dreaming. In her dream, someone walked up behind her and said, "Miss Richcreek." She turned around but didn't see anyone. "Miss Richcreek." She heard it again; then a third time. "Miss Richcreek."

"Hm?"

"Sorry to wake you, Miss Richcreek." It was Officer Nelson. Somehow the dream had morphed into reality. "Did you sleep well?"

"I guess I must have."

"Sorry to interrupt your dreams, Miss Richcreek, but we need the cell."

After numerous blinks, her eyes came into focus. Officer Nelson had a hand on the arm of a young man whose wrists were cuffed together behind his back. It took a minute, but she soon recognized him as the guy she had spent the evening with in the bar. It was Jack.

Once she got her balance, Amarel walked out of the cell. She was still wearing her orange prison jump suit, now in its thirty-fourth hour, give or take a bit. "It looks like you got a search warrant," she said.

"Got a warrant, made a search, and found some interesting items, including several five-dollar bills."

Amarel knew without asking that those interesting bills were brand-new and had consecutive serial numbers.

Officer Nelson continued. "Against your wishes, George got bail set for you. You owe him one dollar. It seems that you are regarded as a minimal flight risk. Your clothes and things are in that box on my desk. You can change in the restroom if you wish."

She wished. *It will be great to get into some normal clothes*, she thought. She was tired of looking like a criminal.

When she came out of the restroom, Officer Nelson said, "You have some papers to sign. Do you want to do that now?"

"If it's all the same to you, I'd like to come back and do that later. Right now I'd rather be outdoors."

"Suit yourself. Just don't wait too long."

She would come back in the afternoon and take care of all that. At the moment, she had a Sunday morning routine to get to. And on this particular Sunday, it did not seem routine at all. After two nights behind bars, everything seemed new and different. In prison, everything is gray: gray walls, gray floors, dingy gray lighting, and a gray smell in the stale gray air. As she walked back to her house, she noticed many things that she had always taken for granted: the smell of the pine trees, the glorious colors of the fall flowers, the myriad shades of green in the lawns and hedges, and the air—the clean, fresh scent of the air. Who knew that ordinary air could smell so good? That was the biggest surprise.

She had to figure out a way to take a shower with two bandaged and injured hands. She finally decided to put on a pair of rubber kitchen gloves. That made the task possible but certainly not easy. Shampooing her hair was even trickier, but it had to be done. There were clots of blood in her hair; she used conditioner, too, knowing that she'd never be able to comb it out otherwise. She combed her hair, had a bowl of cereal, dressed, brushed her teeth, and was out the door.

Then she turned and went back inside.

It seemed advisable to change her bandages. She wrapped her right hand in gauze, which she taped in place. She wanted the gauze to be obvious. It was not a play for sympathy; she just wanted to be sure that nobody would give her a firm handshake. That would have been agonizing.

Out the door she went again. As she walked to church, she enjoyed some more of that delicious fresh air.

When Amarel returned home after church, she saw Hank sitting on her front steps. "Hi, friend," he said.

"Hi yourself. Are you recovered from your ordeal?"

"Not entirely, I guess, but I sure slept well last night. That's a good start. I came to get my uncle's camping gear from your car trunk."

"Good idea. Here are the keys," said Amarel as she gingerly fished them out of her left pocket. She motioned for him to open the trunk.

"What's next for you?" Amarel asked.

"I guess I'll have to try to find some work. What about you?"

"I guess I'll have to take some sick leave until these hands heal up a little."

Sheepishly, Hank said, "I was wondering ... maybe I could take you to dinner sometime?"

"I don't think that's a good idea, Hank. "

They had had this conversation before, and he fully expected that answer, but still the puppy-dog eyes signaled his disappointment. He understood where she was coming from, though. Their worlds had collided, but they were still two different worlds.

"Well, I guess I'll see you around town sometimes. Good luck." He started to walk away.

But Hank didn't know the whole story. Yes, Amarel was afraid that Hank was falling for her. But she was also afraid of her own feelings for him.

"Hank?"

He turned around.

"You can friend me on Facebook if you like. Just search for Amarel. You shouldn't get too many hits."

He smiled. "See ya on Facebook."

CHAPTER 25

SOCIAL MEDIA

For several weeks, Hank and Amarel exchanged messages on Facebook. Neither of them posted very much about their experience together in public posts. The whole thing was so bizarre, how could they begin to tell the story? But in private messages, they briefed each other on their various activities during the following weeks.

"Hi Amy! Thanks for accepting my friend request. I'm busy trying to get my life back in order after all the craziness of the last few days. I hear that Mr. Warren came out of his coma. As soon as I can work up the courage, I'm going to the hospital to see him and apologize."

"I'm trying to get back to normal too. I went back to my outdoor cathedral this morning, I really appreciate the outdoors now in a way I never did before."

"What was the book you were reading in your cathedral? I still don't get this redemption thing. Can you recommend something for me to read?"

"I don't know if he talks about redemption specifically, but I recommend C. S. Lewis. He has a great way of making difficult ideas easy to understand."

"I went to The Bookworm and asked if they had any C. S. Lewis books. The guy said that Amy must have sent me. Did you talk to him?"

"I did not talk to Mr. Stauffer, but he is familiar with my taste in books, so I guess he just assumed. :-)"

"I went to see Mr. Warren today. I figured on doing some groveling, but he was very kind. He even offered me my job back. He said that he had recently lost both of his stock boys. That would be me and Jack."

"That's great that you got your job back. I went into the police station today and signed the last of the forms. I'm 'officially' not a suspect anymore. I guess you aren't either."

"Technically, I'm still on the hook for stealing Uncle Phil's ATV. But he said he'll drop the charges. The only condition is that I have to have his garage window repaired for him. That's a very small price to pay."

"The doctor gave me some hand exercises to do. There was some nerve damage to my right hand, so it needs rehab."

"Guess what? I may be graduating from high school soon. I'm entered in a GED preparation class. They said that my high school records indicate that I can easily get a GED."

"Great to hear about the GED. I know you can do it. No sweat. I had to do a deposition today against Jack. That's like a courtroom testimony without the courtroom. I told them he's the one who gave me the five-dollar bills. They told me that the bartender at Danny Boy's had confirmed my story."

"I got a card from Mom today. Somehow she got wind of our little adventure. She wished me well. It was a nice gesture, I guess. I didn't expect to hear from her until Christmas."

CHAPTER 26

REDEMPTION

A COUPLE WEEKS HAD PASSED. Amarel got up very early that Sunday morning. She went to her outdoor cathedral just as the sun was coming up. She didn't always go there on Sundays, but this was a special occasion. She didn't even know why. It just felt special. She prayed for the secretary of the treasury (he was the next on her list); for her neighbor Sally Reynolds; for the man she had heard about on the news, the terrorism suspect; for Phil and Karen, friends from church who were on a mission trip to Zambia; and for Hank—he was on her list every day now.

After praying, she drove home. She did her normal Sunday-morning routine: shower, eat breakfast, get dressed, and walk to church. She used to drive to church frequently, but now she didn't want to miss out on the few minutes of clean, fresh air that she enjoyed while walking there.

As she approached the church, she saw a familiar figure. At least she thought so. She couldn't be sure from the back. As if on cue, he turned around. It was Hank.

"Howdy stranger," she said.

"Howdy yourself," Hank replied.

Amy asked, "How'd you know where to find me?"

"I didn't. I'm still trying to figure out this whole redemption thing. I figured a church might know something about it. I looked in the yellow pages and saw Redeemer Community Church. Some coincidence, huh?"

Amarel smiled. "I'm not sure there is such a thing as a coincidence. It seems more like a plan to me. Especially since today's sermon is about redemption."

"You're kidding," said Hank.

"Nope. That's the theme for today. I think I have an empty seat next to me, unless you have a better offer."

"I doubt that there could be a better offer."

"You look a little tense," said Amarel. "Is something wrong?"

"I guess I'm kinda worried that everyone will recognize me from TV and think I'm a criminal."

"Stick with me. If anyone hassles you, I'll straighten them out."

As they walked down the aisle, Amarel pointed and said, "I usually sit in this area."

A voice behind them said, "Amy!" Hank turned and saw a balding man, perhaps in his sixties, with a big smile on his face.

Amarel turned around. "Carl!" She gave him a warm hug. "Carl, I want you to meet a friend of mine. This is—"

"I know who this is," said Carl as he smiled and extended a hand. "I'm delighted to see you here, Henry. It is Henry, right?"

"Yes. Henry. Or Hank." He still sounded a little nervous.

"I know you've had some rough times lately, but today's going to be a good day," said Carl.

They received warm greetings from several others, and with each greeting, Hank relaxed a little more.

After a number of greetings, they finally got seated.

Hank thought the music was nice, and there was one song that he really seemed to enjoy:

Jesus, Redeemer, sent from heaven above,
Bringing the message of the Father's love,
Sin had me chained, but Lord, you held the key.
Jesus, Redeemer, you have set me free.

There were prayers, an offering, and responsive reading—the usual church stuff.

Hank was a little fidgety. He seemed interested in the sermon, at least at first. Amarel remembered that he had a short attention span. She prayed that he would hear as much as he needed to hear to get the answers to his questions. The minister was a good preacher, and if anyone could get through to Hank, he could. Just as Hank seemed to be zoning out, the minister caught his attention again.

"I want to tell you about some American heroes," the minister said. Hank's ears perked up. Amarel remembered that Hank was interested in American history.

This church was pretty high-tech. There was a projector that showed pertinent illustrations at appropriate times during the sermon. As the minister spoke, a picture of a postage stamp appeared on the screen—a really old one, from the days when you could send a letter for three cents. The stamp bore the words "These IMMORTAL CHAPLAINS."

The pastor continued. "Their names are Alexander Goode, John Washington, George Fox, and Clark Poling."

Amarel saw no sign of recognition on Hank's face.

The minister continued. "They were extraordinary heroes during World War II. But they were not war heroes. They were heroes of faith. They met each other in chaplaincy training. They had volunteered to serve as chaplains to the soldiers engaged in the war in Europe.

"Rabbi Alexander Goode, Father John Washington, Reverend George Fox, and Reverend Clark Poling—a Jewish rabbi, a Catholic priest, and two Protestant ministers—were being shipped to Europe on the transport ship *Dorchester*. Late at night, the ship was rocked by an explosion. They had been hit by German torpedoes. The ship was going down. The four chaplains remained calm and led the troops to the deck where the lifeboats were located. Some would be saved by the lifeboats, but the ship was overloaded, and not everyone could fit in the boats. The rest would have to depend on life jackets. Every man was supposed to have his own life jacket, but many did not. The four chaplains found a stash of life jackets and began handing them out. But there were not enough. When the supply ran out, one of the chaplains took off his own life jacket and handed it to one of the soldiers. The other three chaplains quickly followed suit. They did all that they could to help the men. Then, when there was no more to do, they climbed to the highest deck of the ship and began singing hymns. One of the last soldiers to make it off of the ship alive told of what he saw in the last moments before the ship slid underwater. The four chaplains had linked arms and were praying—one in Hebrew, one in Latin, and two in English. They were not praying for themselves, but for the safety and consolation of the soldiers in their care.

"In Romans 5, verses 6 through 8, Saint Paul said, 'For when we were yet without strength, in due time Christ died for the ungodly. For scarcely for a righteous man will one die: yet peradventure for a good man some would even dare to die. But God commendeth his love toward us, in that, while we were yet sinners, Christ died for us.'"

The preacher read the verses, which were also projected onto the screen. He continued: "Esau sold his birthright for a bowl of stew. You and I have pawned our birthrights for momentary pleasures, for vengeance, or out of hatred. Whatever our reasons, we were kidding ourselves if we believed that we could redeem our own lives later. Our sins are costly, and we cannot buy our lives back. But there is one who can and who did buy our lives back, even before we were born.

"The penalty for our sins is death—eternal separation from God. But Jesus paid the penalty for us. He took the nails in his hands and his feet, the spear in his side. He took the jeering derision of the people who had hailed him as a king just a week earlier, and even the jeers of the criminals who were hung next to him.

"Perhaps worst of all, he experienced, at least in his emotions, the rejection of Father God, as he cried out, 'Why hast thou forsaken me?'

"Why would Jesus do this? Because we couldn't. We sinners are unable to redeem ourselves. Only the death of the sinless one would satisfy the debt and buy back our lives. The good news is that it is finished. The debt has been paid. Your life has been redeemed, and all you have to do is accept it."

Hank reached for Amarel's hand and gently turned it. Amarel understood what he was doing. She turned her hands palms-up so that he could see the wounds. The left palm was scarred, the right sewn together with stitches.

The preacher went on. "Please bow your heads and close your eyes for the closing prayer. Before I pray, I would ask if there is anyone who would like to receive God's gift of redemption this morning. If so, please simply raise your hand."

Amarel was not following orders. She kept her eyes open a bit to see what Hank would do. He didn't do anything. The pastor prayed the closing prayer, and the organ music began.

Conversations started. Many people greeted Amarel warmly. She introduced Hank to each one in turn. Hank and Amarel then left the sanctuary. On the way out, Hank shook the pastor's hand. Amarel bumped knuckles with him. They had agreed on a safe greeting procedure; no handshakes until her hands had healed.

Amarel stepped onto the grass near the front of the church. Hank joined her.

Amarel said, "I was hoping you'd be ready to respond to the invitation at the end of the service."

"I am ready," said Hank. "It's just that … well … you know that I tend to rush into things. This redemption thing is a big thing, and I just … I want to make sure. There are just a couple of questions—things I want to be clear about."

"Well, come on," said Amarel. "We'll talk to the pastor. I'm sure he can answer your questions."

Hank put out a hand and stopped her. "If it's all the same to you, I'd like to have you answer my questions. You have a way of explaining things so that I can understand them."

"But I don't have all the answers. You know that by now."

"You'll have enough of them."

She saw him looking at her palms again. She paused a moment. "Come on," she said as she put her right hand in the crook of his arm and tugged gently.

"Where are we going?"

"To Maggie's Diner. You're taking me to dinner."

As they walked down the street, she kept her hand on his arm.

Hank said, "By the way, I learned a poem. I want to recite it for you later."

SHE WALKS IN BEAUTY

She walks in beauty, like the night
   Of cloudless climes and starry skies;
And all that's best of dark and bright
   Meet in her aspect and her eyes:
Thus mellow'd to that tender light
   Which heaven to gaudy day denies.

One shade the more, one ray the less,
   Had half impair'd the nameless grace
Which waves in every raven tress,
   Or softly lightens o'er her face;
Where thoughts serenely sweet express
   How pure, how dear their dwelling-place.

And on that cheek, and o'er that brow,
   So soft, so calm, yet eloquent,
The smiles that win, the tints that glow,
   But tell of days in goodness spent,
A mind at peace with all below,
   A heart whose love is innocent!

—George Gordon Byron, 1814

ACKNOWLEDGMENTS

I give thanks to God, who has given me whatever writing skill I may have.

I thank my wife, Beth, who has read and reread this work countless times and has made many helpful suggestions.

I thank Waverly Chadwick, who read an early version of the manuscript and has given much encouragement.

I thank Mark S. Whitcomb, who created the artwork for the front cover.

And I thank all who have read the manuscript and have supported me with suggestions, encouragement, and prayer. These include Linda Griffith, Brad and Mary Barrows, Sandy Megilligan, Dr. Jacqueline Miller, Janelle Sensenig, Rev. Gavin and Christi Whitcomb, Gavin Whitcomb Jr., Fred and Elfreda Holmes, Mark and Debbie Whitcomb, Corey and Joyce Eslinger, Dottie Coulson, Richard Hunn, Janet Batdorf, Julia Newsome, and David Young.

Scripture quotations in this work are taken from the King James Version.

ABOUT THE AUTHOR

Keith Andrew Nonemaker holds a bachelor's degree in mathematics from Messiah College. He and his wife, Beth Nonemaker (née Holmes), are both ordained ministers with Master of Divinity degrees from Bethany Theological Seminary. They have worked as missionaries to Puerto Rico and as pastors. For several years, they were involved in prison ministry at the Dauphin County, Pennsylvania, prison.

Keith has also worked as a teacher. He is currently employed as a computer programmer. His writings have appeared in *The Brethren Encyclopedia, Brethren Life and Thought,* and in several magazines. His writings include articles on church history, genealogy, and computer programming, as well as movie reviews. This is his first novel. Keith and Beth live in Camp Hill, Pennsylvania. Keith is vision impaired and uses assistive technology for his reading and writing.